RESCUED BY LOVE COLLECTION

KALI HART

KAYLEE

RESCUED BY LOVE BOOK 1

1

KAYLEE

"How many friends does that kid *have*?" my sister Lainey asks. Her wide eyes skim the spread of cupcakes covering every square inch of my stainless steel surface.

"A few I guess," I shrug. Finally cool enough to frost and garnish, I pick up the first cupcake and dip my spatula in the blue frosting.

"Two hundred is a *few*?"

Admittedly, this is the largest cupcake order I've ever received for a birthday party. The mass order is the only thing that makes the hour-long drive into the mountains worth the hassle. More often than not, my specialty cake decorating sister sitting across from me receives most of the birthday orders, including the one she's working on now. But this particular customer requested cupcakes only.

"It's at one of those fancy homes with floor-to-ceiling windows overlooking the mountain range," I say as if that explains away the excessiveness of the order. I know because I stole a few minutes in the office with the computer to look it up while Hannah was busy with breakfast pastries.

"Kaylee, we need more cupcakes out here. The case is almost empty!" Eliza calls from the doorway that separates the kitchen from the customer counter.

"On it," I call back.

A timer beeps, alerting me to move the sheets of red velvet, double chocolate, and pink lemonade cupcakes out of the oven and onto the cooling racks. I move quickly, but apparently, not quickly enough.

"Kaylee!" Eliza hollers.

"Do you need my help?" Lainey asks, looking up from the meticulous fondant work she's performing on a princess cake. We all love Lainey's generous, giving spirit, but interrupting her during "sacred custom cake creation time" is something we all know better than to do.

"I got it."

I retrieve a sheet of lemon drop, cookies and cream, and vanilla cupcakes from the cooler, on a mission to refill the nearly empty display case before the second oven beeps a warning at me.

My four sisters and I started the Sprinkles on Top bakery a little over a year ago. We each have our own specialty; mine is cupcakes. To say business has been a booming success is an understatement. The long lines, constant customer traffic, and dozens of custom orders every week attest to that.

"I need three of those red velvet," Becca says from behind the cash register as I rush by with the heavy metal tray. I box her up the request then begin transferring cupcakes into the display case as quickly as I can.

About to head back to the kitchen to grab another tray, a deep male voice stops me. "Is it always this busy in here?" The sharpness in his tone cautions me to take a deep breath and plaster on a smile before I come up to eye-level.

"Pretty much. Isn't it wonderful?" My false smile freezes across my lips as I take him in. All six foot four or five of him. Broad shoulders, chiseled jaw covered with two or three days of stubble, and dark penetrating eyes all packaged in jeans and a button-up plaid. The man is a rugged work of art that has more than a few women in line undressing him with their eyes.

"It's inconvenient."

Mr. Hot Stuff has an attitude. His rude tone takes his appeal down a couple of notches. "It's pretty convenient for business," I say with my smile stretched so wide my cheeks are starting to hurt.

He mutters something undistinguishable under his breath—something about time—as he scrubs a hand through that thick, dark hair. I wonder if it feels as smooth as it looks in the glowing sun. "I need one of every cupcake you got. Sooner rather than later."

With the display empty aside from what I brought out, I know this won't be as hasty an operation as he wants. "I have a dozen varieties, but I'll have to grab most from the back."

I didn't think it was possible for his frown to deepen, but it does. "Do that."

Keeping one of each from the tray, I strut back to the kitchen.

"What's going on out there?" Lainey asks, an eyebrow cocked.

"Rude customer." I roll my eyes as I assemble a Sprinkles on Top box suited for a dozen cupcakes. I could take my time, but the sooner Mr. Hot Stuff gets his order, the sooner he'll vacate the store. Maybe *then* my heartrate will normalize.

"Why are you blushing?" Hannah, who's been holed up in the office handling our social media and marketing since her breakfast pastries were finished, asks. She hooks her purse over her shoulder, headed for the back door.

"I'm not blushing," I say, pulling an apple crumble, strawberry cheesecake, and carrot cupcake from the cooler and placing them carefully in the box. "Just busy."

"Right."

As the oldest, Hannah pays more attention to detail than any of my other sisters. At times, it's a blessing. But right now, it's downright annoying. "What are you doing with the rest of your day?" I ask.

Hannah stares at me long enough to send a silent message. One that implies she's not fooled by my attempt to switch subjects. I divert the uncomfortable glare by turning my back to her and grabbing more cupcakes for Mr. Hot Stuff.

"My only plan," she answers finally, "is to change into pajamas and binge-watch Christmas movies."

"Oh, that sounds fun!" Lainey coos. "Wish I could join you. But I have three more cakes after this one."

"We can't all end our day at ten-thirty," I tease. Hannah is the first of us to arrive every morning at three a.m., and therefore the first to leave.

"Are you coming with those cupcakes?" Eliza pleads from the doorway, strain and pleading dancing in her eyes. "He's already paid and getting *really* upset."

"Be right there. Two seconds."

I grab the last cupcake from the cooler, and seal the box with one of our custom Sprinkles on Top stickers. Back out front, it's not hard to find him. He's standing as close to the *no customers beyond this point* sign as he can without violating any rules, muscular arms folded across his chest.

Good grief, man. I'm doing the best I can. Clearly, he's never worked in customer service. Carrying the box to him, my traitorous gaze sweeps over his tall, muscular frame. Hmm. Maybe a bouncer? With that scowl and his size, it seems like a natural fit.

I offer the box, still trying to place him. I'm sure I've never seen him in here before—I'd certainly remember a man filling out jeans like that. I bet he has those sexy vee muscles that point right to—"Sorry for the wait." I say the words with a sweet enough smile, but there's not an ounce of truth to them. Sexy or not, it's time for the grumpy, rude man to go.

"Took long enough."

It takes every ounce of strength for me to keep my smile in place as he stomps out the door. No need to alarm the customers that I'm three seconds from losing my cool. *What a jerk.* A *hot* one, but still a jerk.

If I never see that man again, it'll be too soon.

2

NIK

Speeding away from the congested bakery, it takes all of two blocks for the guilt to settle in. I was a complete asshole in there. The urge to go back and apologize to the alluring cupcake baker conflicts with the flight I have to catch. I'm already ten minutes behind schedule. Will isn't going to let me hear the end of it if I'm late.

"Jamie, you better appreciate this," I mutter.

My younger sister flies in tonight. She's the one who begged me to pick up a sampling of cupcakes from the local bakery. Though she's still finishing college, Jamie is crazy smart. She has business sense that would put many of the people I've done transactions with to shame.

I promised her if she had a solid business plan—and a degree—I would invest in her startup company. She left the business plan on my dining room table to peak at in between her visits.

Living in the mountains, a drive into town costs me an hour both ways. Even with my lead foot. But Jamie has already reminded me countless times that these cupcakes won't survive sitting in my parked truck all day while I'm out flying around. So, I'm racing back to the house to drop them first.

I keep glancing at my phone in its dashboard cradle, the urge to call the bakery and apologize weighing heavily on me. I'm not the rude type on a normal day, but sometimes that side comes out when I feel under a lot of pressure. The land I need to expand my business might be sold to my competitor before the day is out if I don't act fast.

I'll lose signal in roughly three miles.

More than anything, I yearn to hear the baker's voice. Maybe if I hadn't been a giant pain in the ass to her, I might've had the courtesy or sense to ask her name. The image of her is burned into my mind. Those sparkling blue eyes, lips reflecting a hint of gloss, and her curvy figure. Curves I yearn to run my hands over.

I shake away the thought and drop the idea of calling the bakery when the bars disappear from my phone.

I'll never see her again. It's only for Jamie that I drove so far to pick up cupcakes in the first place.

My stomach rumbles as I rush into the house to stick the box in the fridge. I flip open the lid and help myself to a cupcake with white frosting sprinkled with crushed cookie crumbs. *Delivery fee.*

The first bite stops me in my tracks. The sweet treat is soft, rich, and an explosion of flavor. I regret scarfing half of it in one bite. Damn, this is delicious.

I hurry out the door, licking frosting from my fingers as I back out the driveway. I'm in a hurry to get to the small airstrip to meet Will. I fear that if I stay too close to home for another minute, Jamie might not have any cupcakes for her experiment.

"Thought you weren't gonna make it," Will jabs when I meet him outside his Super Cub. The plane is big enough for the two of us to sit up front, and three passengers in the back. But the only one coming with us today is his German shepherd, Grizzly.

"Had to run an errand in town. Thanks for waiting."

Will is one of my good buddies, someone I can call in a pinch and count on to show up. He's my go-to pilot when I want to scout out a parcel of land for sale. I own a bunch of fishing cabins that can only be accessed via plane or a long four-wheel trek into the mountains.

Grizzly gives out a bark from behind as the plane takes off. I turn and scrub my hand along his neck. I catch myself wishing Ms. Cupcake Baker was sitting in the back of the plane, coming with me to see this property.

I shake away the odd desire. I've been on my own for a while now, ever since my ex took off with a guy I thought was my friend. I don't trust easily. Life is simpler without a woman to complicate it. My decisions aren't clouded by emotions.

"Look deep in thought there, Nik," Will ribs as we approach the lake matching the map I was given.

Ignoring his prodding, I point to the water below. "I think that's the piece. Get a little closer?"

"Sure thing."

The chatter on the radio is lost to loud thoughts in my head. The guilt of my rude behavior must be the reason I can't stop thinking about *her*. But as much as I try to convince myself that's the answer, a gut feeling tugs me in another direction.

"We better hurry," Will says, pulling me back to the present. "Sounds like severe weather is rolling in."

From this high up, the wall of darkening clouds in the distance is unmistakable. "One more circle around the lake, then we can head back."

I should be contemplating whether to make an

offer on a piece of property I was never able to step foot on. Instead, all I can think about is how desperate I am to see her again. Desperate enough to attempt another cupcake run in a crowded bakery and risk her wrath. I *have* to see her again.

3

KAYLEE

The sprinkles of rain that dusted my windshield when I left town have turned into heavy, thick raindrops. They fall faster with each mile. When I turn off the paved highway and onto the dirt road, my GPS alerts me that I'm four miles from my destination.

The narrow, winding road is littered with puddles and a couple of branches the gusting wind has knocked down.

Eliza warned me about the incoming storm when I loaded up the two hundred cupcakes in my SUV. "Can't you drop those off in the morning?" she asked.

Technically the birthday party isn't until tomorrow. As the rain falls in heavy sheets, I wish I'd braved the call to the overzealous mother to push out the delivery time. But selfishly, I wanted my day off tomorrow. I only get one a week.

Fingers curled around the steering wheel in a death grip, I crawl along the steep muddy road, cautiously swerving around puddles and debris. With less than two miles to go, headlights flash in my rearview mirror.

Some jerk in a massive truck is on my bumper seconds later.

I've had just about enough of being pushed around today. I stick to the middle of the road that's less likely to suck in my tires into the muddy slope of the ditch, despite the incessant honking behind me. "Give it a break already, buddy!"

I bounce hard in my seat, held down only by my seatbelt. A crunching of cardboard and plastic from the back threatens the condition of my cupcakes. The wheel jerks in my hands as I try to figure out what the hell just happened. I was so focused on the rearview mirror that I missed what was right in front of me. But judging by the wobbly steering, I think I blew a tire on one of those puddles. I jab a finger on the hazard light button and ease over as close to the shoulder as I dare.

Letting out a heavy sigh, I free my phone from its dashboard cradle. "No signal. Of course not."

The truck that was on my ass the whole way up

the hill has stopped behind me. He's either going to help me, or kidnap me and chop me up into little pieces out here in the woods. But if I wait in my car for the rain to stop so I can walk back to the highway to call a tow truck, it might be morning.

None of my sisters were expecting to hear from me again tonight. After this cupcake delivery, I had exclusive plans with a bubble bath, bottle of wine, and a steamy book. I'll have to take my chances.

I jump at the knock on the window. I can't make out his face through the heavy streaks of rain. I look around for a weapon should I need to defend myself. All I have is a plastic serving utensil, but it *does* have a pointed end.

At a second knock, I roll down the window.

"Are you—you again?"

The deep, sexy voice is at once recognizable. My core tingles before my brain can remind it we don't like Mr. Hot Stuff. "What are *you* doing out here?"

"I live out here."

Of course he does. His rudeness makes more sense, as only people with excessive amounts of money live off this mountain-view road. I'm not saying money makes *all* rich people snobs, but I've certainly met more than a few since we opened the bakery.

"You blew a tire," he adds when I don't say anything.

"Because *you* were on my ass. What was with all that honking anyway?"

"I was trying to warn you."

"About what?"

He points straight ahead. "That." A massive tree stretches across the road hardly twenty yards ahead. Had I hit that...I shudder at the thought. Even at the slow speed I was traveling, the collision would've been brutal. How the hell did I not see that? "Oh."

"What're you doing out here anyway? Don't you know we're in a flash flood warning?"

"*In* the mountains."

"Yes. They happen here more than you might think. You shouldn't be on this road right now."

Thank you, Mr. Obvious. "I have a delivery. Well, had." For the first time since the accident, I dare to turn my head over my shoulder. Though I can't get a clear view of what happened in the back of my SUV, the smeared blue frosting on my ceiling doesn't bode well for the order.

Tears well in the corners of my eyes.

"I live right over there," he says, pointing up the hill to a massive log cabin style house. "You can come in and use the phone if you want."

I wish I was in a position to say no to Mr. Hot Stuff. He's caused me enough trouble today, yet my stupid nipples still react to his voice. It's not fair for a man to be so irritating and irresistible all in the same moment. "Let me—let me check the damage."

"I told you," he says, backing up so I can push open my door, "blown tire."

I dash to the back of the SUV and open the hatch. Three cupcakes roll out and splash into a puddle. It looks like a blue frosting bomb exploded in my car. Cupcakes are everywhere. One drops off the inside of the hatch and smacks me in the face.

"You ready?" He shouts now that the rain is pelleting us both.

I tuck my purse under the crook of my arm like a football and brave the rain. Mr. Hot Stuff is kind enough to close the hatch for me as I make a mad dash for his truck. I sit in the passenger seat, feeling completely defeated by this day.

The second I get home, I'm running that bubble bath. Or maybe I'll just open the bottle of merlot and drink straight from it. Screw the cute glass with the words *World's Greatest Cupcake Baker* etched into the side with dozens of little hearts.

"I haven't caught your name," he says, pulling away from the wreckage and heading toward a winding driveway even higher up on the hill, just short of the fallen tree.

"Kaylee," I say with a heavy sigh. "Kaylee Belmont." If I had *any* energy left, I'd ask him his name since I'm tired of calling him Mr. Hot Stuff in my head.

"Kaylee, I want to apologize for being such an ass this morning. I was in a hurry, but that's no excuse.

Jamie wanted the cupcakes, and now she won't even be able to fly in until tomorrow."

A twinge of jealousy shoots through me at the mention of another woman. A girlfriend or wife? His ringless finger isn't enough to answer that uninvited question. I shouldn't care that he has someone in his life. In fact, it should make me feel relieved. I can finally be free of this ridiculous crush I've had on him since the moment I laid eyes on him.

"It's fine," I say, accepting his apology. He *is* more or less rescuing me right now. "We all have our days Mr.—"

"Paxton. But call me Nik."

Somehow, knowing his name only makes him hotter. *Nik Paxton.*

Going home with him, however brief, is probably a bad idea. But I don't try to stop him from driving away from my poor car and up his driveway to his lavish house.

4

NIK

"Any luck?" I ask Kaylee when she hangs up the phone for the third time.

"No. Sounds like the road is closed. No one can get here until tomorrow morning *if* the storm passes." A crackle of thunder emphasizes her point.

"You're welcome to stay here." A heated look passes between us, causing my pulse to double. The image of Kaylee naked beneath my sheets flashes through my mind, forcing me to turn away and busy myself with wiping down the already clean kitchen counter. "I have a guest room. Three actually. You can have your pick."

"Thank you." I hear the first crack of her tough

exterior in that defeated tone. "I don't really have anywhere else to go."

"I promise I'm not some bear *all* the time," I say in attempt to lighten the mood. "Don't tell anyone, but I have a soft side too."

"You?"

I turn back around to meet her blue-eyed gaze. A man could get lost in that trap for eternity. "Oh yeah. I've even been known to *like* cupcakes. May have even sampled one this morning."

"I thought you said they were for *Jamie*." The way she says my sister's name has laughter bubbling my stomach. I know we just met today, but there is definitely jealousy there. *Good.* I don't want to be the only one who feels this irrationally strong pull between us.

"My sister's delayed from the storm."

"Ah, Jamie's your sister."

"Who did you think she was?" I ask, a teasing edge to my voice because I already know the answer. The blush that creeps up her neck and settles on her cheeks is cute as hell.

"Your girlfriend."

"Don't have one of those." The dim light reveals a smudge of blue on her cheek. Because licking it off her soft skin might alarm her, I wet a towel and hand it over instead. "You have a little—"

She uses her reflection in the window over the

kitchen sink to wipe it away. "Thanks. I must look like a hot mess. Soaking wet, covered in frosting."

Hot mess? Hardly. But I *have* been thinking about getting her out of those wet clothes since the moment we made it inside. "Well, there are cupcake crumbs in your hair."

"Figures." A smile warms her lips at my banter. I've been trying to break down those ice-cold walls since I discovered her on the side of the road. Although the apology I owed is out of the way, I still feel like I need to do more. As if having Kaylee Belmont upset with me is more unacceptable than anything else in my life.

I cross my arms and lean back against the counter, afraid that if I leave my hands free, they might betray me and reach for her. The impulse doesn't make any sense, but it's there nonetheless. "You said you were delivering an order?"

Kaylee lets out a groan. "Two hundred cupcakes. Birthday order."

Everyone on this mountain road knows each other, and I can only assume it's for Mrs. Bradley and the boy she spoils rotten. I should be shocked at the amount, but honestly, the kid gets everything he wants to excess. "Well, I doubt there'll be a party today."

"It's tomorrow. I guess I better call her and tell her what happened. I hate to ask my sisters to make a new order, but what other choice do I have?"

"Make them here." The offer is out before I can rein it back in.

"*You* have baking ingredients? In bulk?"

The only reason my kitchen is loaded with baking supplies is because Jamie bakes nonstop when she's home. She's set on opening a gluten-free bakery, but not until she can get the taste to be as close as possible to the real thing. It's the reason she wanted professional cupcakes waiting for her upon her arrival.

Opening the door to the pantry, I wave for Kaylee to step inside. "See for yourself."

She gasps when the light flickers on. "*This* is your pantry? It's like a mini supermarket in here. What are you doing with all these baking ingredients anyway? Don't tell me *you* like to bake."

"Me? Hardly. My sister dabbles. She's only home one weekend a month, so I like to keep her well-stocked." Somehow, I don't think it'll win me any points with Kaylee if I tell her I might be funding future competition for her business.

I wait as Kaylee skims the pantry, silently ticking off items as she finds them. It gives me the opportunity to take in the sight of her body. Jeans plastered on her legs, a button-up shirt rolled up to her elbows, the blue top beneath it revealing cleavage that makes my mouth water. I don't have to stare to determine her tits are perfectly bountiful. I bet they'd feel great in my hands.

"Wow, I'm impressed. You just might have every-thing I need to make two hundred cupcakes. Even the food coloring. You're not secretly trying to run me out of business, are you?" She teases.

I give a hearty laugh, but I don't outright answer. "Did you want to put on some dry clothes?" I ask, changing the subject. "I can lend you something to wear."

"That would be nice, actually. I'm a little over my clothes clinging to my skin."

I'm not. "Be right back."

Alone in my bedroom, I steal a minute to catch my breath. I command my speeding heartrate to slow and my half-hard cock to tame. Kaylee's only staying because she has no other option. Though she's warmed up to me, that doesn't mean anything more.

I change into a pair of mesh shorts that'll better hide my misbehaving dick.

Digging through my dresser, I shake away thoughts of getting involved with the cupcake baker. The only room I have in my life for a woman is Jamie, and I'm happy to keep it that way for the fore-seeable future.

"You didn't tell me I also had frosting in my hair," Kaylee accuses when I return to the kitchen with a t-shirt and sweatpants for her to change into. An array of baking ingredients is spread across the island, along with a variety of baking dishes and utensils. It reminds me of having Jamie home, except Kaylee is much more organized. "Mind if I shower?"

"Not at all." I turn so she can't see me gulp a swallow at the thought of her naked.

KAYLEE

"Step away from the cupcake batter, or I'll get you with the flour," I warn Nik playfully, waving a spatula at him.

"I can't sample it?" he pouts. Though it's exaggerated, it's another sexy expression he wears so well. That genuine smile though, the one he lets out when he's got his guard down, is my favorite.

"*After* I've filled the pans." I'm still shocked that he coincidentally had all these ingredients in his pantry. I wonder if anyone else on this mountain had found me if they'd have been able to offer the same. *Doubtful.*

"Okay, okay." He goes to the fridge and pulls out the box he picked up from the bakery earlier today. "I'll steal one of Jamie's. She's not here to stop me."

I ladle batter in a practiced rhythm I've perfected over the years I've been making cupcakes, long before my sisters and I ever went into business together. I'm thankful the task is something I can do on autopilot, because Nik has proven quite the distraction. "Do you just have one sister then?"

"Yeah. Jamie's in college." He selects the red velvet and returns the box to the top shelf of the fridge. It gives me a peek at his abs when his shirt lifts. "It's just been the two of us for the past few years. Lost both my parents within a year of each other."

"I'm sorry to hear that." The similarity to my own parents is eerie. "We lost my mom to cancer almost a decade ago and my dad to a heart attack two years later."

"You and your sisters?" Even the way he eats that cupcake is sexy.

"Yep. There's five of us altogether." I feel my pesky heartrate start to normalize as I ramble on about my family. It's the easiest topic for me to get carried away about, other than cupcakes of course. The man I was too happy never to see again this morning is making it eerily easy to hold a conversation. One that has substance.

If he'd come into the bakery as this version of himself, I would've been a puddle of goo.

"What made you decide to open a bakery together?" he asks, leaning on the island.

His cologne drifts over the aroma of cupcake batter, rendering me momentarily speechless. When my ability to speak returns, I say, "We each had our own side hustles and specialties and other jobs on top of it. Eventually it ran most of us into the ground trying to keep up with it all, so we decided to combine forces and bet on ourselves."

"Wow, that's an impressive story." I don't know when it happened, but Nik moved from the opposite side of the island to mine. He leans closer, reaching for the abandoned spatula resting in the empty bowl. "I'm impatient."

One step closer and our bodies would graze. I could reach up to his stubble-covered cheek and draw him down for a kiss I've been thinking about nonstop. This morning, I considered us enemies. Now that darkness has fallen, I see Nik in a different light. For the first time, I'm glad the heavy rain hasn't let up.

With any luck, the storm will rage all through my day off. I'm not in a hurry to leave anymore.

"Any good?" I ask as Nik licks the spatula clean.

He reaches across me for the bowl, his arm grazing my breasts. My entire body responds with electric tingles. "Mmm hmm."

Pans of uncooked cupcakes sit on the counter, ready for the second preheated oven. But I can't seem to move my hands toward them. I'm too entranced by the way Nik inhales the cake batter. I want to taste it on his tongue.

"Kaylee, if you keep looking at me like that..."

I bite down on my lip. "Like what?" I reach my hand toward his lips, wiping away a splatter of cake batter and licking it off my own finger.

He drops the bowl and spatula on the counter in a clatter and pounces forward. Our bodies tangle together as his lips collide onto mine. I open my mouth, inviting his tongue to tango with mine. I was right. He *does* taste like vanilla.

Hot hands run up and down my sides as the urgency of the kiss grows. He works at the hair tie holding my half-dry locks in a bun. Damp hair falls around my shoulders. "I like you with your hair down." His dark eyes are heated with passion as he comes in for another series of steamy kisses that cause my nipples to stand at attention.

I can't remember the last time a man kissed me and made me feel so...*alive*.

I'm so glad I was wrong about Mr. Hot Stuff this morning. *So. Damn. Glad.*

Our heated make-out session is interrupted by a timer, announcing a batch of cupcakes is ready to come out of the first oven. "I got them," Nik says, pulling them out and setting them on cooling racks I'm thankful I set up an hour ago. He doesn't bother to put in more sheets, and I don't either. *They can wait.*

"Now, where were we?"

Our bodies mold together in perfection. My breasts press up against his hard chest as my fingers claw the hem of his shirt. I'm dying to feel the sculpted muscles I know he's hiding beneath it.

His sweatpants, already loose on my curvy hips, make it easy for Nik to slip a hand inside them. "If you want me to stop—"

"Are you kidding me?"

He laughs a low, devious rumble against my neck as his fingers slide to my wet center. "I bet you taste even sweeter than your cupcakes." Nik kneels, sliding the sweatpants down to my knees. Thanks to the rainstorm, I'm panty-less and completely exposed to him.

If this rainstorm is somehow the end of the world, then so be it. I have no regrets.

As Nik nudges my legs wider, I grip the lip of the granite island and hold on for dear life. His hot breath teases my aching core. It's pleasureful torture in its best form, but I swear if the man doesn't put his mouth on me *now*, I'm going to put my pussy there myself.

"Looks like I'm not the only impatient one." He wiggles his eyebrows up at me, looking sexier than ever between my legs.

"Eat me."

"Gladly." His mouth covers my pussy as his masterful tongue explores my folds. His stubble rubs the inside of my thighs. "Mmm," he moans against me, the vibration intensifying every sensation. I slowly rock my hips against his mouth as his hands cup my ass, pulling me tighter against him. It's a wonder the man can breathe.

"Oh!" I cry out, my release growing closer with each magical motion he performs down there. "Nik, I'm going to come." It's the only warning I give him before my pussy starts to convulse against his face. He holds me tight against him, keeping his mouth firmly in place until my body stops shaking.

"I was right," he says with a wicked smirk on his lips. "You *do* taste sweeter than your cupcakes."

6

NIK

We've definitely crossed a line we can't come back from now. The taste of Kaylee's sweet pussy remains on my tongue as I help her finish baking the two hundred cupcakes. Though the clock warns us it's getting late, I know the night is far from over.

"I can drive you up the road to the Bradley's in the morning to deliver these," I offer.

"I thought there was a tree blocking it."

I'm addicted to watching her hips sway, my sweatpants hanging low on them, as she moves about the kitchen finishing up her final tasks. Too bad I can't experience this every night. "If it's still there in the morning, I can take a back way."

"That dirt road isn't the backway?"

"That's the main road."

Kaylee wipes down the counter after the last of the ingredients are put away. All that remains now is what she'll need to mix frosting in the morning. "You'll have to apologize to Jamie for me. I ran you out of baking powder."

"I'll pick up some more." Unable to resist having Kaylee in my arms, I move across the tile floor until I'm standing in front of her. I twirl a strand of loose hair around my finger, eager to free it from its bun again now that the baking is done for the night.

"Thank you, Nik. For...well, everything." The gratitude sparkling in her eyes warms my heart. I want to see that all the time. From Kaylee. She's strong and confident. More than capable of taking care of herself. But I still yearn to be the one who rescues her when life drops too many obstacles in her way.

I could fall in love.

Hell, maybe I already have.

"If you want a guest room, I'll make one up," I say, giving her the option to leave what we started to fizzle out.

Her fingers reach for my hips, fiddling with the waistband of my shorts. Her soft skin feels like silk. "What're my other options?"

I close the slight gap between us, gently pressing my erection against her stomach. "We both get naked. In *my* bed."

"I like that one better."

"Good." I pull her hard against me, nuzzling her neck. I don't know what tomorrow brings, but Kaylee is part of it. I know it in the depths of my heart—a place I'd considered dormant until I walked through the door of Sprinkles on Top.

Our clothes are missing by the time we make it to my bedroom.

"*This* is where you sleep?" Kaylee's eyes widen, likely at the size of the master bedroom. "This room is bigger than my apartment, and I share that with Becca."

"Stick with me babe," I say playfully, admiring the full glory of her naked body. "You ain't seen nothing yet."

She drops her gaze to my erect cock, purposely staring at me for several seconds. Lust fills those baby blues as she bites down on that lip. It drives me crazy. "After *that*, I'm sure I've seen it all. It's a good thing I'm off tomorrow."

"Why's that?"

"I doubt I'll be able to walk after tonight."

Backing her up to the bed, Kaylee drops onto the mattress. Her bountiful tits bounce as I hover over her, demanding my attention. I palm them both as we shimmy to the top of the bed, taking one nipple in my mouth, then the other.

"Do you want me to use a condom?" I ask, not

even sure the box I have is valid anymore. It's been a while since I've been with a woman.

"No."

"I was hoping you'd say that." I kiss a trail from her nipple to her lips. "I want to feel *all* of you."

"Me too." Our gazes lock, more than lust dancing between us. Something much more powerful than chemistry. I swear I see my future there. I've never been a man who believed in fairy tales or soulmates, but it wouldn't be the first time I was wrong about something.

She guides my cock to her center, those soft fingers driving me wild. They feel so good, wrapped around my length. Her pussy feels even better. I slide into her slowly, fighting the urges to ram into her.

At her gasp, I still. "You okay?"

"Yes, Nik." She lifts her hips, helping me go deeper. "I'm better than fine."

Our lips crash together and her fingers dig into my shoulders. "Faster," she pleads. Together we rock harder. Her wet channel squeezing my thrusting cock is the definition of euphoria. I want to capture this sensation and experience it forever.

"Can I get on top?" she asks in a pant.

"Gladly." We roll, our bodies never losing the connection.

Kaylee grips my shoulders, those tits hanging just above my mouth. I can't resist taking one into my mouth as she controls the pace, thrusting and grinding. The look of ecstasy is etched on her face. She's biting on that bottom lips again.

"You feel so *good*, Nik."

"Ride me, babe. Ride me until you come on my cock."

"I want you to come with me. *Inside* me." She rocks harder and faster, damn near sending me over the edge in a heartbeat. It takes every ounce of control to hold my release. I wait to fill her with my seed until she's writhing on my cock.

Together, our worlds explode in bright, powerful colors and sensations.

"Fuck, Kaylee. That was amazing."

"You're telling me."

The words I want to say—*I think I love you*—remain strangled in my throat.

7

KAYLEE

I've never frosted two hundred cupcakes naked before, but I have to admit it's kind of fun. Nik made a rule that clothes were not allowed before seven-thirty. "What about coffee?" I ask, almost halfway through the spread. It might be a while before Sprinkles on Top has blue-frosted cupcakes in their case.

"Coffee is not only allowed, but required." Nik walks by me on his way to the coffee maker, sticking his finger in my frosting bowl.

"Hey, not until I'm done Mr. Hot Stuff." My cheeks instantly heat at the nickname I never intended to tell him he had.

"What did you call me?" He's barely able to ask

the question through his laughter. Blue frosting lingers on his fingertip as he approaches. "Mr. Hot Stuff was it?"

"It's what I called you before I knew your name."

Nik laughs louder, and I have to admit the sound is gloriously heartwarming. Man, I could get used to this. I haven't given much thought to dating in the past couple of years since my cupcakes business started to boom. When we opened our bakery... dating just got put on the backburner. But now, I want more. I want Nik. "You called me Mr. Hot Stuff even when I was a total prick?"

"I didn't say it was a term of endearment."

"Oh, really?" Before the frosting-covered finger can reach his mouth, he changes his mind and swipes it across my boob.

"You're lucky I have a hundred more of these things to go or you'd have blue frosting on your cock."

"You'd have to suck it off," he says, his dark eyes promising he's only half-teasing.

"What the hell?" I stick my finger in the bowl and smear a blue line over his dick.

The morning is a blur of passion. Me sucking his cock, Nik feasting on my pussy—my personal favorite—sex in the shower, and a final round in the bed before the ticking clock warns me I need to finish the cupcakes and get them delivered.

With reluctance and wobbly legs, we find

clothes. I keep extra boxes in my car, and Nik is kind enough to retrieve them after a promise that a buddy of his is on the way to tow my car to his driveway and fix the blown tire.

I know we just met, but I love the way Nik takes care of me. He doesn't treat me like I'm some delicate flower incapable of handling my own, but he's not afraid to step in and handle things to ease the burden.

I think I'm in love with him.

No, I *know* I am.

Visions of our future have pushed their way into my mind with such persistence that I've given up fighting it. Steamy nights, naked baking, mountain views, and some day, a crew of kiddos to complete the picture.

"They got that tree cleared off the road. Ready to get these cupcakes dropped off?"

"Yeah."

Nik stops short of the door, spinning. He draws me into his arms and kisses me deeply, making my toes curl. "What was that for?" I ask, nearly breathless when our lips finally part.

"Just because."

Nik's truck has little problem making the two-mile trek higher up the mountain. Mrs. Bradley is tickled with delight at the timely delivery despite the bad weather and includes a very generous tip. One I'll share with my sisters.

"I want to see you again, Kaylee," Nik says on the drive back to his house. From the road, I can see his buddy fixing my tire. Day off or not, I have obligations in town. Things I need to take care of before another brutal six-day streak. My schedule is one of the reasons I haven't pursued dating. I don't know how to fit it in.

But for Nik, I'll figure it out. "I'd like that."

He squeezes my hand in the driveway. "Dinner. Tonight. I'll pick you up at seven."

"Okay." Fighting the wide grin would be pointless, so I don't. "I need to grab my purse from inside."

"I think Mitchell's just about done. I'll help him finish up."

Even our soft kisses make my nerve endings come alive with feeling.

I take my time inside, wanting to commit not just the house, but also the love we made to memory. I know it's way too soon to admit how I feel. But I'm excited to know we have a future waiting for us. The possibility of forever. The *I love you's* can come later.

"Where's my purse?" I mumble. My search takes me from the kitchen, to the pantry, to the bedroom, and through the dining room. I spot it resting on the table, uncertain how it got there. I scoop it up, ready to hurry outside when something beside it stops me in my tracks.

A binder labeled *Jamie's Sweet Treats* showcases a cupcake logo. Nik mentioned Jamie dabbled with baking, but he didn't imply anything beyond that. I shouldn't look, but my curious fingers flip the binder open.

"A business plan?" I carefully turn the first page and discover a map. One that includes the down-town strip of my town. A big red X is placed across the street from Sprinkles on Top.

"Kaylee, you ready? Your car's done." Nik calls from the kitchen. "Kaylee—" He stops when he finds me in the dining room, binder in hand.

"What is this?"

"I can explain."

"Your sister is going to be my *competition*? And you knew about this?"

"It's not what you think. I promised Jamie if she had a business plan and a degree that I would invest—"

"You? *You're* funding it?" My hands shake with rage. Yes, I'm furious with Nik, but mostly I'm angry at myself for being so naïve. What normal man keeps a pantry fully stocked and ready to whip up two hundred cupcakes at any given moment? How did I not see right through that lie for what it was?

"Kaylee, wait."

I keep going until I'm in my car, relieved to find the keys inside. I roll the window down when I see Nik running up to me. "I don't want to hear it. You *lied* to me. Have a nice life, Nik. Don't call me."

8

NIK

"Did you at least tell her that I want to open a gluten-free bakery?" Jamie prods over a takeout dinner. She's been busy in the kitchen baking, and I've been battling a competing offer for the land I want to purchase.

The past two days have been hell. Jamie has been on my case about moping around.

"Nik?" Jamie says in pushy voice.

"No, I didn't. What difference would it make?" Kaylee will forever be convinced that I'm the bad guy. Better to count my losses now before I get in too deep.

"You love her," Jamie says matter-of-factly.

Except, I already *am* in too deep. "Give it up,

Jamie."

"No." She grabs my truck keys off the hook and rushes for the door. "Either you come with me to tell her how you feel, or I'll just do it for you."

I scowl at her as I shove my wallet in my pocket and follow her out to the truck. "Who taught you how to play so dirty?"

"*You* did."

The hour-long drive gives Jamie plenty of opportunity to coach me on what to say, but all of her words of wisdom go out the window when we pull up in parking spot in front of the bakery. I can see Kaylee at the front counter, smiling at a customer as she hands over a box of cupcakes.

I wipe my sweaty palms against my jeans. I've spent two days convincing myself this was never meant to work, but seeing her unravels that lie.

I need Kaylee more than I need air.

"Well, what are you waiting for?" Jamie pressed. "Go in there."

I'm drawn to Kaylee, even through the storefront glass. The magnetic pull between us in undeniable. She looks up before I can reach the door handle, confirming my suspicions. We're connected.

Her smile drops to a scowl. "You're not welcome here," she says in a low but firm tone.

Two women stand on either side of her, their arms crossed. I see the family resemblance in their facial features and the way they can level a man with powerful narrowed glares. "I love you," I blurt, completely forgetting everything Jamie told me to say. But I know it wasn't to start with *that*.

One sister softens her expression.

"I'm sorry I didn't tell you about my sister's bakery plans. She's still a semester away from graduating college."

"She wants to put a store across the street from us," Kaylee snaps.

"A *gluten-free* bakery."

"Gluten-free?" The less-scowly sister repeats. "Kaylee, that's actually not a bad idea. We don't offer any gluten-free sweets. How would that be *bad* for business?"

"If you want to talk to her, Jamie's out in the truck. But I didn't come here to discuss business. I love you, Kaylee. That night with you was the best night of my life. I want that *every* night. With you."

"Oh!" Both sisters soften at my declaration. "Go talk to him!"

Kaylee lets out a deep breath then moves around the counter, keeping her arms folded across her chest. "You can't keep secrets from me, Nik. I don't need a relationship built on lies and dishonesty."

My heart thumps happily in my chest as she drops her arms and takes a step closer. "I own a bunch of land and a remote fishing cabin business. Might also be a good time to mention that I'm loaded."

"Anything else?"

I feel completely at ease at Kaylee's non-reaction to my admission of wealth. "Only that I love you, but I think I mentioned that already."

"You just met me," she challenges.

I gather Kaylee into my arms, brushing her cheek with my palm. "I dare you to tell me you *don't* love me."

"I can't."

When our lips finally meet, the sisters behind the counter and the few customers in the store all start cheering like we're in some romance flick. But I don't give a damn. All is right with the world now that Kaylee is a part of it again.

EPILOGUE

ONE YEAR LATER...

KAYLEE

"Becca, when are you going to ask that poor man for his phone number?" I ask my sister after the man she's been drooling over for weeks leaves the bakery with his son.

"He's not my type."

I run my hand over my swollen belly as I move around her to check the cupcake situation in the display case. Not surprising, it's low on vanilla bean, strawberry cheesecake, and double chocolate—both regular *and* gluten free.

"Keep telling yourself that lie, Becca. Maybe one of these days you'll convince me. But today is not that day."

"He wouldn't be interested in me," she says,

fiddling with the business card rack in front of the register. Blush creeps onto her cheeks. Those two are hot for each other, I'd bet my cookies and cream cupcake recipe on it.

"You really think that with the way he was looking you up and down?"

"Kaylee, do we need more gluten-free cupcakes?" Jamie calls from the doorway to the kitchen.

"You're lucky," I say to Becca. "But this conversation isn't over." I move around her, finding it more challenging to maneuver through the narrow space now that I'm carrying our first child. I still have three months to go and can only imagine the challenges I'll encounter in this cramped space. My sisters and I have toyed with the idea of finding a bigger space, but for now, it's a pipe dream.

"We need more double-chocolate," I say to Jamie.

"On it."

Ever since she graduated college, Jamie came up with a business proposition my sisters and I couldn't turn down. Instead of opening her own store, she rented space in ours. We sell her gluten-free cupcakes right along with our own line of treats. She has her own logo on her trays. We even offer deals for buying combination orders.

Though I was skeptical at first, I'm glad we took a chance on her when she moved to town. She's brilliant when it comes to business sense, and a very talented baker.

Seconds after I've refilled the display case, Nik struts through the door to take me home after a long day on my feet. He looks sexy as ever with his debonair smile that warms all my insides. "Guess I'm off," I say to Becca, untying my apron and dropping it in the bin beneath the counter.

"Hey, babe." Nik pulls me into his arms and kisses me deeply in front of everyone. He's never afraid to show affection, no matter where we are. I think it might be his way of marking his territory, but I don't mind. Not one bit.

"Miss me?" I tease when our lips break apart.

"Always."

He kisses me again, more passionately this time. His lips move to my ear. "Since we have the house all to ourselves tonight, I think we need to make some blue frosting."

BECCA

RESCUED BY LOVE BOOK 2

1

BECCA

It's Tuesday.

The best day of the week.

It's the day that Soren and his son Luke stop by the bakery for one of my cookies.

"Your *boyfriend* is here," my sister Eliza teases, nudging me with her elbow.

My pulse jumps when I spot them outside the glass door. "He's not my boyfriend," I hiss under my breath, worried the customer she's helping might overhear. But the sweet, elderly woman seems oblivious to our conversation.

"You should do something about that," Eliza says with a nod up front as Soren holds the door open for his son. "*More* than trying to impress his son with your cookies."

Each of my sisters and I have a specialty we bring to our bakery: cupcakes, donuts, even ice cream. Mine is cookies. "I don't know what you're talking about," I say seconds before my eyes connect with Soren's. My entire body tingles with excitement.

His smile is dangerous.

Panty-incinerating dangerous.

Every woman in town fawns over Soren Atkinson. It's not just his sinfully hot looks—the man could be a movie star with his Greek-god body and killer smile. It's how he is with his son that melts most of our hearts right into a puddle of goo.

Eight-year-old Luke is Soren's whole world. Seeing the two of them together is sweeter than any cookie I have to offer in our case. But I refuse to be just another woman, tripping over my own feet, just for a chance to catch his eye and say hello.

"Hi Miss Becca!" Luke's face lights up the second he bolts through the door and charges toward the counter.

I'm supposed to be in the back right now prepping tomorrow's cupcakes since my sister Kaylee is on maternity leave. But I wouldn't miss my Tuesday with Soren and his son for the world. I've already accepted that I'll be working late into the night to make up for it. Not like I have plans to be anywhere else. "Hey Luke! I have a brand new cookie for you to try today. If you're brave enough, of course?"

I feel Soren's gaze land on me. I let my own flicker up to his hazel eyes briefly. *Friendly customer service.* At least, that's the lie I tell myself every Tuesday. His smoldering expression and those damn eyes have my neck flushed and panties drenched. This reaction has happened every week since he started coming to Sprinkles on Top.

"I'm brave!" Luke declares. "Right, Dad?"

"Bravest kid I know." The way Soren says it, he means it. *Dammit.* It makes my heart soar and nipples tighten. Later tonight, I'll let a bubble bath, some candles, and a glass of wine set the mood for my Soren-filled fantasies. "So, you're *not* scared of monsters, right?"

Luke giggles. "No!"

I know the question is safe because the kid is obsessed with those Pixar monster movies. In fact, he's the inspiration behind my creation. Every week he comes in, he always has that monster-themed backpack bouncing behind him. "Good. Because this one is a *monster* cookie."

"A *monster*?" Luke's expression morphs from skeptical to excited the second he spots the tray in the display case. "Cool!"

"Monster, huh?" Soren repeats, a mischievous twinkle dancing in those beautiful eyes. I think I've been caught. I'm overheating, and I know it's not the ovens. Only half of them are running since I'm up front and *not* making my sister's cupcakes.

I move behind the case, aware of Soren's searing gaze following me. It's all I can do to keep my hands steady as I lift the tray to give Luke a better view. My sisters swear the man is interested in me, but I think otherwise. He hasn't dated since he moved to town over a year ago—at least not that anyone knows. This is a nosy town. *Someone* would know.

I think they're mistaking Soren's friendliness for interest. I know better.

He could have any woman he wants, and no matter what my sisters tell me, he's *way* out of my league.

Of course, that didn't stop me from wearing a new red dress with white polka dots that showcases the girls without being sleazy. I've already caught him stealing a glance once, and it makes me yearn for his hands on me. I may not be his type, but he *is* a man.

Soren leans on the top of the case, his gaze dropping to my cleavage a second time before it flickers up to my eyes. I feel like he's about to ask me something. Something important. "Can we see that green monster cookie?"

I hide my embarrassment beneath the case, realizing that Luke has already picked out his favorite. *See?* I want to yell at Eliza who keeps throwing me wiggly eyebrows and suggestive winks.

"You're sure this is the one?" I ask Luke, holding it out on a napkin for him to assess. I've made similar cookies before loaded with peanut butter and M&Ms. But I've never topped them off with green frosting and a quirky monster face made of candy and frosting designs.

"Wow! Dad, this one's so cool. Can I have that one? Can I please?" Luke's enthusiastic approval warms my heart. Someday when I settle down and have kids of my own, I hope they're like him.

The image of Soren, Luke, and me living in a house together with a couple more kids flashes through my mind, deepening the flush that refuses to fade in Soren's presence. "I'll box this up," I say, eager for an excuse to spin around and hide my face.

"You're the best, Becca," Soren says. The way my name sounds on his lips causes my entire body to heat and tingle. I've had the biggest crush on Soren since the first time I met him. I might even be in love with the man. Pathetic, I know.

"Here you go." I hand the box to Soren, gasping when his fingers graze mine. It's not fair how a single soft touch can make my pulse race. Maybe it's better this way. To never share more than these simple Tuesday exchanges. I might spontaneously combust if the two of us ever got naked together.

"Thank you, Becca." He's in no rush to pull his hand away. Not until Luke demands to hold his prize. "I guess we better get this wrapped up," he says to me, apology in his eyes. "Luke's spending the night at Grandma's and we're already a little late."

"See you next Tuesday?" My smile stretches so wide my cheeks hurt.

"Count on it." He winks at me from the front door, but I wait until it closes to release the breath I held.

"Friendliness my ass," Eliza mutters.

2

SOREN

Every Tuesday is the same since Luke and I moved to town. After the drama and heartache we went through with my ex-fiancé, this small piece of our routine is refreshing and grounding. One cookie a week gives him—and me—something to look forward to. Something he can count on.

Luke spends Tuesday night with my mom to bond with the grandma he's hardly known, and to give me a break. Between the grueling hours fixing bush planes and hauling Luke to and from school and activities, I get worn out.

But I wouldn't trade our new life for the world.

Over a year ago, I promised my son we'd get a fresh start. Just the two of us; no women.

It's the only reason I haven't asked Becca Belmont out on a date.

At the stop sign leaving my mom's neighborhood —she moved to town a few years ago and promised we'd be happy starting over here—I sit a few seconds longer than necessary. If I turn right, I head the short drive outside of town to my cabin.

If I turn left, it'll take me by Sprinkles on Top.

I've had a mad crush on Becca since the first time I saw her behind that counter. Award-winning smile, dazzling blue eyes, and a curvy figure that could give a man a heart attack. Her kindness is genuine and her cookies are amazing.

In a different set of circumstances, preferably one that didn't involve my ex wreaking havoc in our life, Becca would've been the woman I chose. I wish I'd moved to town sooner and avoided that last mistake completely. If only I'd known Becca was in this quaint town just outside the mountains...

I turn left, despite my better judgment.

By now, the bakery is closed. Driving by it this late proves nothing except that I'm a lonely, desperate man.

I perk up when I notice a light on inside. My pulse jumps as I catch a flash of a red dress through the window just before it disappears into the kitchen.

That dress nearly broke me today. The sight of it

on her amazing body clouded my senses. I almost asked her out in front of Luke.

My heart swells, remembering how his eyes widened with such excitement at the *monster* cookie. I should stop. Tell Becca just how much I appreciate what she did for Luke. Because I *know* she made these special cookies for my son.

I'm in a parking spot outside the bakery, slipping my truck into park, before I even realize what I've done.

The door's probably locked.

It doesn't stop me from getting out of my truck. I don't see Becca through the glass front windows now, but a glow emits from the doorway to the kitchen. *Is she here all alone?* Despite my speeding heartrate, I frown. I don't like the thought of her here, all alone, this late. What if someone breaks in?

Reaching for the front door, I'm surprised to find it unlocked.

"Becca?" I call out, wondering if perhaps she's hosting some kind of private cookie decorating party in the back. Maybe that's why she didn't secure the door. But the absence of cars outside suggests otherwise.

I step all the way inside when she doesn't answer. The hum of fans and dinging of an oven time likely drowns out my voice.

There's still time to turn around. It's the last sensible thought I have before I approach the counter and lean over it. "Becca, are you still here?" I call, catching a blur of red and several dozen cupcakes filling the counter. *Not cookies*?

Becca appears in the doorway, nearly tripping over her feet as she jerks to a halt. Her blue eyes go wide at the sight of me, but it's the way that her tits bounce in that damn dress that makes me incapable of speech. "Soren? How did you get in?"

3

BECCA

My heart thunders in my chest at the sight of Soren inside the bakery. It's not just that I *swore* I locked that door. It's Soren *freaking* Atkinson. In the bakery with me. Alone. So very alone.

"Sorry to stop by unannounced," he says, that deadly smile tugging at his lips. "I saw the light."

"Where's Luke?" No way the man stopped by without his son. He's never done that before during business hours. Why would he now?

"I dropped him off at my mom's. Tuesday night tradition."

It takes a few seconds more, but my feet finally remember how to function and I shuffle around the counter toward the front door that shouldn't be unlocked. Sure enough, it is. I fish the keys out of my pocket, prepared to lock us in before I realize what I'm doing. "Oh, did you..."

"Do you always leave your door unlocked?" Instead of heading toward the exit, Soren leans an elbow against the counter. This man *had* to be a model in some former life. What I wouldn't give to learn all about him and his mysterious past. "Becca?"

"I thought it was locked," I say, remembering he asked me a question two solid minutes ago. I lift the keys toward the door again and drop them. Though the idea of locking the two of us in a bakery together *is* tempting, I'm not sure Soren would enjoy being held prisoner. "Did you need more cookies?" I ask.

"No," he answers with a low, deep laugh that strikes me in the core. Dammit, I only brought *one* change of panties to work today. I don't have another. "I wanted to tell you how much I appreciated the monster cookies. I know you did them for Luke."

Heat flashes up my neck and settles on my cheeks. He caught me. "Got the idea from that backpack of his," I say, hoping he won't figure out just how much effort and thoughtfulness I put into the idea. That might be stepping across some invisible line. "He liked his then?"

"The kid was *still* telling my mom about his awesome cookie after dinner when I left."

I can't hide the enormous smile that spreads

across my lips. It's the highest form of compliment a customer can give me. Each new cookie creation is special to me. Like releasing a part of me into the world for everyone to judge. "I'm glad to hear that," I say.

I'm confused why Soren hasn't moved from the counter. "I hate to rush you," I say, meaning those words to their full extent, "but I'm covering for Kaylee this week. I have a couple hundred cupcakes that need frosting for tomorrow's display case."

Leisurely, Soren pushes off the counter. "Would it make you uncomfortable if I asked to stick around for a while?"

My heart pounds so hard against my chest I think it might pop out. I'm thrilled and...confused. "You're more than welcome to stay," I say, managing to calm some of my nerves. "But I have to ask ... why would you want to?"

Soren shrugs his broad shoulders. "House gets a little quiet without Luke there. Thought it might be nice to have some company. And honestly, I'd feel better knowing you made it home safely."

That last part makes me feel all warm and gooey inside. Maybe Eliza is right. "I'm locking you in. Last chance to bolt."

Soren laughs again. "Take me prisoner."

I spin around so he doesn't see the instant flush to my face. Oh, I'd take him all right. Any way he'd let me. On top. On the bottom. Bent over the counter. "You can't tell my sisters I let you in the kitchen."

"It'll be our little secret."

I feel that heated gaze on my body as he follows me into the kitchen. These panties are toast. What I need to do is frost these cupcakes. I still have over a hundred to go. But now that I have an audience, I'm nervous. Cupcakes—including the décor—are Kaylee's thing. "Do you want to watch me butcher frosting these cupcakes, or do you want to watch me do something I'm actually good at?"

He arches one of those damn fine brows, so much innuendo there I nearly squeak my question.

"Like make a batch of cookies?"

"I vote cookies. But only if I get to lick the beaters."

The image of him working that tongue gives me pleasureful shivers. I bet he can do amazing things with it. "Since I've put all my cookie ingredients away for the night," I say, putting cupcakes on trays to frost later—who needs sleep?— "I'll need some help getting them back out."

Soren gives me that dangerous wink. "I'll earn my keep."

As I lead him back to the storeroom, I try to tamp down the fantasies of making out back here. I've dreamt about it more than once, wishing a Tuesday would give me just a few minutes alone with him.

I prop the heavy door open with a bucket of

frosting. "I'll need some flour, sugar, salt, the usual. But the special ingredients hide out on that top shelf." I point to a shelf I can't reach with even my fingertips if I stretch up on my toes. I could use the step stool folded in the corner, but what fun is that when I have all six foot five or more of Soren to aid me?

"This is quite the storeroom," he says. "You're not planning to *sleep* here tonight, are you?"

I follow his gaze to the cot behind me. "Oh, that? No. We put that in here when Kaylee got further along so she could take power naps."

"Reminds me of a bunker."

"Cot, world's tiniest bathroom, and all the sugar you could ever want. I think it'd pass for surviving an apocalypse."

Soren laughs, that dangerous smile lighting up his face and revealing his darkening eyes. "You're funnier than I thought," he says, his tone all compliment. He reaches up with ease and hands me a bag of chocolate chips. "I guess I don't get to talk to you much on Tuesdays."

"It *is* a little hectic." This might be that opportunity Eliza keeps insisting I'm squandering. The one to ask Soren out. Or at least for his number. But the words are trapped in my throat. Despite the way Soren's intense gaze sweeps down my body and back up, I'm still fearful of rejection.

I'm suddenly warm. *Very* warm. I shuffle backwards, chocolate chips in hand. "Maybe we should get started on those cookies," I say, careful to avoid grazing his arm with mine. As much as I long for his touch, I'm afraid what it'll do to me.

"Need anything else? Salt you said?" He reaches a hand over my shoulder toward the shelf, causing me to panic.

I hop backwards. My heel kicks the bucket of frosting hard enough to shove it outside the door. I trip over my own two feet—literally—and my ass pushes the door closed. *Shit.*

"What's wrong?" Soren asks, no doubt because my eyes are wider around than my cookies.

"We're locked in."

4

SOREN

"Locked in?" I repeat the words Becca said, certain there's something I'm missing.

"Yeah." Her head, and her smile, drops. The urge to draw her into my arms and reassure her everything will be fine overwhelms me.

The desire inside me to make this woman happy every moment I can for the rest of my life is *burning* inside me. I can't make any sense of it, or where such a powerful feeling came from, so I don't even try.

"Soren, I'm so sorry. It's one of those bomb shelter doors. You can only open it from the outside."

I place my hand on her bare shoulder, my traitorous gaze dropping to her cleavage. We would be trapped together with Becca in that fucking hot dress. I've been able to resist her for months. But tonight, I might be a weak man. *I have to get us out of here.* "Let me try it."

She steps out of the way, the fronts of her tits sliding across my chest. My dick twitches in my jeans, but because of the close quarters, I don't think she notices. "I don't think there's a way to open it," she says.

I tug on the handle so hard I fear I might break it off. It's definitely locked, and with its design, there's no way to pick it either. "Got your phone?" I ask, realizing that I left mine on the counter next to the cupcakes.

"In the kitchen." Dread lingers in her soft blue eyes, tearing at my heart.

"Hey, it's no big deal. I'm not the worst guy you could be stuck in here with, right?" I flash her the smile that makes her flush, hoping to lighten the tension.

"But Luke—"

"Is with my mom all night. She'll be taking him to school in the morning. As long as we can get out of here before I have to pick him up in the afternoon, I'm good." I take a couple steps closer to Becca, going slow to see if she backs up from my approach. The last thing I want to do is frighten her.

"Hannah comes in at three," she explains.

Oddly, disappointment is the first feeling that

strikes me. Considering it's nearly ten now, five hours doesn't seem like enough time to spend with Becca. I should feel panic, because five hours is *too* much time for me to get into trouble.

Unable to resist the urge any longer, I tug her gently into my arms. Becca falls against my chest, her head tucked beneath my chin. "We'll be fine for a few hours," I say. "I promise I won't bite—unless you want me to."

"Don't tease me," she says with a laugh. "I might take you up on it."

I've suspected for weeks that Becca might have a thing for me. But the monster cookies she made for Luke today confirmed it. I've been fighting my feelings for her for so long...would it be so terrible to give in?

"How sturdy is that cot?" I ask.

"Sturdy and *comfortable* enough for a nine-month pregnant mother."

I take her by the hand and lead her the short distance to the cot. "Let's sit." What I really want to do is lay her down on the cot and push that dress up. Slip my fingers between her wet folds and find out how sweet she tastes. But I'm more of a gentleman than that. "You from here?" I ask, sitting beside her. Our thighs touch, but I don't bother trying to put distance between us.

I'm losing my fight to resist her with each passing

second. If it weren't for the promise I made Luke, I wouldn't fight it at all.

"Yeah, my sisters and I all did. Boring huh?" Becca wets her lips with her tongue, driving me crazier than she could possibly know.

"Not at all. I like this town. It has enough going on to be interesting, but it's quiet too. Friendly."

"Where were you at?" she asks, fingers fiddling with the hem of her dress. "Before you moved here?"

"New York." The admission tastes sour on my lips. I don't even like the person I was before I moved here. I was so focused on making money that I almost married the wrong woman. "Tell me about your cookies."

"I'm not giving away any secret recipes," she teases.

I'm so damn relieved for the easy change of subject. "When did your cookie obsession begin?"

The corner of her mouth quirks up at my description, but I just smile back.

"I was five," she says, letting out a happy sigh and leaning back against the wall. I join her, unable to keep my eyes off her tits. The way they lift as she squares her shoulders—it's like they're begging to be squeezed. If I don't sit on my hands, I might just grab them. "My mom—she passed away several years ago —she taught me how to bake them."

"She taught all of you?" I ask.

"Yeah. We definitely inherited our love of baking from her." She shifts against the hard wall.

"That can't be comfortable, Becca." I lift my arm and draw her against my chest. Damn she feels so good against me. I try to convince myself it's just having a woman in my arms again that feels this way, but really, it's her.

"We each kind of gravitated toward our own thing. But cookies were mine. I got a little mean about it, too."

"You *mean*?" I shake my head. "I can't imagine it."

"You haven't tried to come between me and my baking." She lifts those baby blues in my direction, licking her lips again. All I can think about is kissing her. Tasting her. Devouring her mouth.

"I wouldn't dare." They're the last words I manage, because Becca lifts off my chest and turns her head toward me. All the feelings I've battled for weeks rush forward, making it impossible to fight this any longer.

When her soft fingers graze my cheek, I lean in for the kiss I've craved.

5

BECCA

I'm kissing Soren Atkinson.

This can't be real. But if it's a dream, no one better wake me up. I don't care if I'm passed out on the cold metal table with frosting in my hair.

His wondrous lips move against mine in the perfect way I fantasized they would. This first kiss is everything I imagined it could be and more. So. Much. More.

Soren's strong arms wrap around me, pulling me tighter against him. I rake a hand through his hair, curling my fingers against the back of his neck. Closer. I want him closer. I part my lips, inviting his tongue to dance with my own. I taste a hint of frosting, and it makes me smile. "Those cookies aren't just for Luke, are they?" I murmur against his lips.

"He shares." His hot hands curl around my neck and slide over my shoulders. My breasts yearn to be touched, squeezed, fondled by his large hands. "Becca," he says, pulling back from my lips but descending on my neck.

"Yeah?"

"I have a confession."

I stiffen, fearing it's something terrible. Like he's still married. Or gay. But no way in hell is this man gay and handling a woman like *this*. "Rip the band-aid off," I plead as his lips move across my shoulder.

"You assume it's something bad?"

"Isn't it?"

His laughter vibrates against my sensitive skin. "Only if *you* think it's bad."

Our gazes lock, revealing the desire drenched in his darkened eyes. "What is it?"

"I've wanted you for a long time," he says, maintaining eye contact with every word. Eliminating any chance that he's just a horny man taking advantage of the woman he's trapped with for the next few hours. This man is telling the truth. I'd bet my monster cookie recipe on it.

"You're not the only one with a confession," I say, though my words come out more as pants now.

"Oh yeah?" His warm hands move up and down my bare arms, warding off any chill the storeroom had to offer when we first entered. His gaze dips, meeting mine squarely. "Rip off the Band-Aid," he whispers against my cheek.

"I've had a crush on you, too." I'm not about to admit that it started the very first day I saw him. That sounds a little...stalkerish. But it feels good to get this off my chest. No matter what tomorrow brings, at least my sisters will get off my back now.

"Have you now?" One hand slides down my arm and drops onto my leg.

"Don't act like you didn't know." I attempt an eye roll, but damn his touch is clouding my senses.

"I hoped," he admits.

I'm dying to know what held him back, but as a palm flattens against my breast, I decide to save the burning question for later. Right now, I want to be ravaged by my crush while the opportunity is here. I don't dare think about tomorrow, and what might change when Hannah unlocks that door.

Our lips meet again, sensual yet hungry. Urgency builds as he squeezes my boob through the pesky fabric. It's a great dress to show off the girls, and yielded the attention I was after from Soren, but not so great to invite roaming hands inside. It's much too tight for that.

I reach behind my back and tug the zipper down.

"Oh my, Becca." He scoops his hand inside, massaging my breast and teasing my nipple. Best thing about this dress: no bra.

It feels so damn good to be fondled. My eyes fall closed and I lean back to give him better access to what he wants.

"Any cameras in here?"

"No." Even if there were, I wouldn't let it stop anything that's about to happen. I have the password to the security footage memorized. I could erase the feed if it came down to it—or make a personal copy first. *Too bad.*

"Good." He slips my dress straps off my shoulder, exposing my breasts to the chilly storeroom air. But my pebbled nipples are all from anticipation of what Soren will do with them. "These are so nice, Becca." With both hands, he kneads the girls. Our lips reconnect, beginning another round of an even hotter make-out session.

I've never had a man worship me quite like this before. Add that it's Soren, and I'm dizzy with pleasure. This is already every fantasy I've had rolled into one. But I still want more. I reach for his crotch, my palm connecting with his hard length. There's nothing small about this man, including what he's hiding beneath those jeans.

"Becca," he growls my name against my lips as my fingers work at his zipper. "You're sure about this cot?"

I dive my hand inside his jeans and find the opening in his boxers. "Guess we'll have to test its stability rating."

"Is that a challenge?"

Squeezing his cock, I say, "Maybe it is."

"Then I think I need to get you out of this dress." Soren pops to his feet, tugging me with him.

Panic falls over me as I search for the light switch. But before my fingers can reach it, Soren covers my wrist. "Leave the light on. I've been waiting too long to see you naked to miss a single moment."

The way he says those words, like a hungry lion about to devour its prey, shakes away my self-conscious fear. I have generous curves that aren't always thought attractive, but Soren's gaze drinks me in as I let the dress fall to the floor. I stand before him in nothing but a pair of silk panties.

"Fuck, you are so hot, Becca. Every last amazing inch of you."

I no longer question *if* I'm in love with this man. I *know* I am.

6

SOREN

Becca stands before me, naked and exposed aside from her black panties. I'm stunned by her beauty and her curves. *Claim her.* The voice whispers in my ear, almost an order. Not to bury my cock in her once, but forever.

I shove away the thought. I can't think beyond right now. Because that requires talking to my son and getting his permission first. Whatever happens in this storeroom has to be a secret from Luke. But I *will* broach the subject of dating Becca with him.

As eager as I am for what's about to happen, I already know one time will never be enough.

"If you don't get your clothes off, I'll do it for

you," Becca says to me, yanking me back into *this* moment.

I lose my shirt, jeans, and boxers, kicking them off to the side. I stand naked before the woman I could so easily fall in love with, if only I let myself. My hard cock yearns to be inside her. To claim her as my own.

With two steps, Becca's in my arms again. Our lips know the way to each other already as our bodies press together. Her soft skin against me is the best feeling in the world. I let my hands roam up and down her body until they stop at her panties. I'm tempted to get them off, but it might be fun to leave them on for a little while longer.

I dive inside those panties, slipping my fingers between her wet folds. She's so fucking wet. I saw my hand against her pussy until she's whimpering. But I'm not ready to take her over the edge just yet. I pull down her panties. "Lay down for me, babe."

The cot's not big, but it's bigger than most I've seen. Sturdier too. But I don't want to test its limits with Becca on her back. After I eat her out, we'll have to figure out another position.

"Soren—" Panic flashes in those eyes as I drape her legs over my shoulders.

"What is it babe?"

"I—I haven't...I've never had a man—I'm not a virgin, but—"

"You've never had a man lick you before?"

"No."

"Good." The jealous side of me is fucking tickled to know I'm the first man to taste her sweet juices. "Then let me show you what you've been missing." I descend on her pussy, covering it with my mouth. Though I'm hungry and eager, I take my time with my tongue. Tracing the dips and folds with leisure.

"Oh—oh!"

Finally, her tense legs relax and Becca lies back. "Just enjoy this, babe. It's all about you right now." Though eating this sweet pussy is as much for my enjoyment as hers. Fuck she tastes so good.

When her hips start to buck, I pull her thighs against my shoulder and increase the intensity of my suckling. My tongue weaves its way through her pussy like its been given a lethal dose of caffeine.

"Soren—I think—I think—oh!"

The noises she makes when she comes are so fucking sexy. They'll plague my dreams for many nights to come. I hold my mouth against her cunt, willing her to come on my face. When her body finally stills, I come up for air. "How was that?"

"*That's* what I've been missing?" She brushes away the wild locks of red hair that have shaken loose from her bun, a glowing smile illuminating her face. So damn glad we left the lights on.

I want to tell her that I'm the only man who'll ever put my lips to her center, but it's not fair for me to make that claim. *Not yet*. But I know once I'm inside her, I won't be able to stand the thought of another man coming after.

"I want inside you, Becca."

"I want that too."

Pushing off the cot, I reach my hand to help her up. I draw her into my arms, kissing her. Allowing her to taste herself on my lips. A gentle kiss turns hungry. My throbbing cock demands entry.

"I'm going to take you from behind," I say. "Is that okay?"

"You can take me any way you want." That dreamy, orgasm haze fills both her words and her hooded eyes. Fuck me, I think I'm in love.

7

BECCA

My legs are shaky after that insane orgasm. I've never *let* a man go down on me before, but I can't for the life of me understand why. The feel of his tongue teasing my clit, his lips covering my pussy...and that orgasm...*best one ever.*

"Turn around, Becca," Soren says. "I need to be inside you."

I'm not a virgin. I've had sex a few times, but I've never enjoyed it. It's one of the reasons I threw myself into this bakery business when my sisters and I decided to open Sprinkles on Top. It gave me an excuse to avoid dating and having bad sex with guys I didn't really like.

But with Soren...I don't think it's possible to have bad sex.

I turn away from him, searching for the best option in the tight space. A wooden cabinet about hip-high offers the best handhold. I grip the sides and wiggle my ass in invitation to Soren. He steps behind me, sliding his massive cock between my legs.

I'm terrified he's going to split me in two. But there are worse ways to go...

I forget I'm afraid when his dick slides between my sensitive folds. When his head rubs against my nub, I moan. "Oh, I like that."

"Just wait," he promises.

He moves his cock to my entrance and pushes inside. I lift on my toes, offering him access. I bite down on my bottom lip through the initial pinch of his entry, but any pain subsides to pleasure in seconds. My channel is so wet and ready for him. My walls stretch to his size within a few thrusts.

"You okay, Becca?'

"More than okay."

He rocks in and out of me slowly, burying himself as deep as he can go with each stroke. "Becca, I have a confession."

"Another one?" My teasing tone comes out as more of pant.

"If I come inside you, you'll be mine. Only mine. I can't share you."

His words make my entire body tingle. "Promise?"

It's all the permission he needs to steadily increase the pace. Words are lost to the overload of pleasure that builds. I desperately want him to slam into me, but I don't rush him. Regardless of what he says, I know tomorrow isn't promised. He might think differently about me when we're not trapped alone together.

I shove away the thoughts, memorizing how amazing it feels to have Soren filling me. Completing me.

"Come inside me," I plea as the pace grows hungry; savage even. He pounds into me harder with each thrust until he cries out and stills. There's no better feeling than his cock filling me like this. It feels meant to be—far beyond some silly crush. This...this is true love.

8

SOREN

With Becca in my arms, my world feels complete in a way it hasn't in a long time. Hell, maybe it's *never* felt this way. I hope and pray that Luke is on board with this idea, because I don't know how I'd live without her.

Worse, if Luke's *not* okay with me being with Becca, we might have to stop coming to Sprinkles on Top. I don't know if I could bear to see the woman I love day after day, remembering how fucking amazing it felt to be inside her, and know we can't be together.

The storeroom has grown chillier as the night's gone on, which forced us to reluctantly get dressed. I left my shirt off so Becca could use that as a blanket.

"You comfortable?" she asks with a yawn.

"I'm perfect." The cot's a bit tight, but it gives me every excuse to hold her extra close.

"You sure?"

I kiss her temple. "Relax, babe."

"Soren?"

"Yeah?"

"Why have you never asked me out before?" When I don't answer right away, she adds, "You said you've had a thing for me for a while. You had to know I was single. What held you back?"

Well shit. I guess the conversation has to happen now. "It's Luke."

"He doesn't like me?"

"Are you kidding? You're his new superhero after that monster cookie." Softly, I caress her arm through my t-shirt blanket. "We moved here after a bad breakup. Luke was devastated to lose another woman in his life. He lost his mother to a car accident when he was four."

"I didn't know that. I'm so sorry, Soren."

Her genuine sympathy warms my heart, melting the last of the ice I'd kept as a shield. "I promised Luke when we moved here that we would start a new life, just the two of us. No women."

"Ah, I see." The flatness in her tone twists my heart.

I inhale deeply, searching for the right words so she'll know that this wasn't a one-time deal for me. I want to make this work. But before I get to chance to say anything more, the door pops open.

"Whoa!" Hannah Belmont's eyes grow three times the size. "What—you know, never mind."

"We got locked in," Becca explains, jumping off the cot like it caught fire. She hurries out of the storeroom without looking back at me. I want to believe she's just embarrassed her sister caught us off guard. By my watch, she's an hour early. But it doesn't explain the dread that fills me.

"You're lucky I'm here," Hannah says to Becca as if I'm not lurking in the storeroom, putting my shirt back on. "You didn't even get the cupcakes *frosted*."

"Hard to do when you're locked in a storeroom without a phone," Becca fires back.

Fearing my phone might hold unanswered texts or calls from my worried mother, I'm forced to slink into the kitchen to retrieve it. As I reach for it, Becca's sister points a spatula at me.

"What are *you* doing here?" She shifts her narrowed gaze to Becca. "We don't allow anyone who doesn't work here into the kitchen. Family rule."

"He's leaving," Becca says. Turning her head toward me, she adds, "Right?"

It feels wrong to leave things this way. Without further explanation or even a goodbye. But Becca has already started frosting cupcakes. "I'll see you later, Becca." I linger, hoping she'll look up at me. It feels wrong to end our night this way.

"Door's unlocked," Hannah adds when she notices I haven't budged.

"Right. Goodnight ladies."

BECCA

"You've been moping around the bakery for a week!" Eliza scolds. "You're going to scare away all the customers."

"Ha ha." I give her an exaggerated eye roll, but she's not wrong. This has been the longest week of my life, and the first Tuesday I can remember dreading. I have no clue if Soren and Luke will come in today. Maybe they'll find a new Tuesday tradition. And if they do show up... I let out a heavy sigh.

"See!" Eliza points at me. "You're doing it again."

Discovering a wadded up rag beneath the counter, I use it to wipe down the back of the display case. "Am not." I stick out my tongue, feeling like we're kids again. But I know Eliza's only pushing because she cares.

"Have you talked to him?"

After Hannah found Soren and me in the storeroom all cuddled up together, tangled arms and legs, it was hard to hide it from the rest of my sisters. Even Haylee knows, and she's still at home. "What would I even say?" Soren made it pretty clear that he has a pact with his son. I would never ask him to break it so we could be together. "I don't want to come between. Surely you get that?"

"I do." Eliza has a daughter from a heated high school prom night. She hasn't let a man get close in years. And never close enough to meet Amelia. "But Luke *likes* you, Becca. That's different."

"Is it?"

"I guess you're about to find out." She nods discreetly at the front door.

My heart flops around like it's drunk in my chest at the sight of Soren and Luke. I have no fucking clue how I'm supposed to act, so I do my best to paste on a smile and treat this Tuesday like any other that came before it.

Except the hint of Soren's cologne in the air reminds me of him between my legs, feasting on my pussy. His smile, however, isn't quite so potent today. I'd venture to say it's a bit sad. I already tried convincing myself he's a jerk and a player, but I know he's not. He just loves his son. How can a girl fault him for that?

"Hey Luke."

"Hi Miss Becca!" Luke charges toward the counter, leaning both arms against it. "Got any new cookies today?"

"I do have one new one. It's called a lemon drop."

Luke's adorable face screws up in the way I expected. "Lemon?"

A smile breaks across Soren's lips, drawing my gaze to them. I miss the way they felt against mine. "I know it doesn't sound too exciting. But sometimes you have to take a chance. You don't know if you like something unless you try it, right?"

Luke ponders what I said for a few seconds. "Okay. But if I don't like it, can I pick a different one?"

"Luke," Soren scolds.

"Of course you can." I retrieve one lemon drop cookie from the display case and hand it over on a napkin.

As Luke skeptically breaks off a piece and studies it, I dare to look at Soren. So many unsaid words linger between us, but now is not the time. Not with his son in company. I want to ask him to call me later and even consider jotting my number on a napkin.

"Wow," Luke says, his expression morphing into joy. "This is really good!"

"See?" At least this little boy can warm my cold

heart today. *Small victories.* "Sometimes you just have to take a chance." I pull two more cookies from the display case and slip them in a small box. "These are on me today. You boys enjoy." I wink at Luke, but I'm too intimidated to look at Soren again. The sooner they leave, the sooner I can move on. Accept that Tuesdays will be all we ever have.

"Thank you, Miss Becca!"

"You're welcome."

"C'mon, Luke." Soren puts his arm on his son's shoulder and leads him toward the door.

But before they get there, Luke stops. "Dad, you promised."

"You're sure, bud?"

"I like Miss Becca."

Eliza grabs onto my arm so tightly her fingers cut off my circulation. "Oh my god!" she says to me in a whisper shout. "This is just like a movie."

"What are you—"

Soren spins back toward the counter, reaching across it for my hands. His eyes bore into me until I look up. "I never meant to lead you on, Becca. What we shared...that wasn't meant to be one time. I wanted it to be much more than that. But I wasn't sure how Luke would feel about me dating again."

I'm too stunned for words, and terrified to get my hopes up. But I give Soren my full attention knowing he wouldn't say anything in front of Luke he couldn't take back.

"I've fallen for you." The pleading, sincere look in his eyes does me in. I effectively melt into a puddle of goo. I think Eliza does too from the sounds she's making. "I've fallen so hard—dammit, I'm in love with you Becca Belmont. I think I have been for a very long time."

"She loves you too!" Eliza squeals. I turn a severe look at her. "What? You told me you did."

"You're okay with this?" I ask Luke.

He nods enthusiastically through a bite of his cookie.

"What if..." I look at Soren, "what if this doesn't work out?"

Soren hops over the counter like it's not even in his way and gathers me into his arms. "It'll work out, Becca. Because I know you're the one for me. The one I've been meant to find all along."

His words make me feel like my entire body is soaring above the clouds. "Okay."

"Okay?"

"Let's do this then. I love you, Soren. I'm all in if you are."

"Always." He scoops my chin, lifting my lips toward his, delivering a kiss filled with promise and love. When our lips break apart, he whispers against my ear, "I'm home alone tonight. Unless you spend it with me."

EPILOGUE

BECCA

"It's your turn, Eliza," I say again from behind the front counter of Sprinkles on Top during a lull of customers. Soren, Luke, and our baby girl Amanda will be here soon. But I'm not letting up until then.

"I'm happy for you Becca. You married an amazing man who treats you like a queen. He loves his family more than life itself. But that fairytale...it just doesn't exist for me. I accepted that a long time ago."

"Why not?"

She lets out a frustrated sigh. "You know why."

"High school was a long time ago. Amelia's almost ten now. You deserve to find love, too. And I won't stop being pushy about it no matter how much you threaten to sabotage my cookies."

"You're wasting your time. I'm through with all that. No more love. No more bad boys. No more men!"

"Some of them give really good orgasms." I wiggle my eyebrows at her.

"Oh yes they do," Kaylee says, patting Eliza on the shoulder as she walks by with a tray filled with cupcakes for the display case. "Wait until you meet the right one. You'll change your tune really quick."

Before Eliza can object any further, the bells jingle over the door—we installed those after Hannah learned I forgot to lock the bakery that night Soren and I got stuck in the storeroom. I don't know why I bother wearing panties on Tuesdays. They all suffer the same fate the second this man walks through the door and flashes that dangerous smile my way.

"Got a new cookie today?" Luke asks, enthusiastic as ever.

"You know I do."

Luke's little sister watches with fascination from Soren's protective embrace. I've never admitted to any of my sisters that my daughter was created in our bakery storeroom. Somehow, I don't think they'd appreciate that fun fact the way I do.

"What do you think?" I ask Luke after he takes a test bite.

"So good!"

Untying my apron, I drop it into the bin. "Guess you're off the hook for the rest of the day," I say to Eliza with a wink.

I move beneath my husband's outstretched arm and let it pull me in against him. "Hey there baby girl." This is the first time Amanda will join her brother at Grandma's house for a Tuesday overnight. I'm torn, but I'd be lying if I said I wasn't looking forward to a night all alone with my hubby.

Soren kisses my temple. "I have plans for you tonight, Mrs. Atkinson," he says low against my ear. "None of them involve sleeping."

ELIZA

RESCUED BY LOVE BOOK 3

1

ELIZA

"We need more sprinkles!" one of my sisters calls from the front.

I frantically search the storeroom, certain I stashed one last canister on a top shelf. For reasons I can't quite figure out, our little town suddenly has a sprinkle shortage. I've been sourcing online options, but most of them are a rip off. I have one shipment on its way, but it'll be the end of the week before it gets here.

"Eliza?" Lainey hollers.

"Got it!" I hop onto a step stool, swipe the bottle, and hurry back to the front. I hope this canister will last until then.

We've had to improvise on sprinkles for most of

the baked goods these past few days, but when it comes to the homemade ice cream—my specialty— people come to the Sprinkles on Top bakery *for* the sprinkles.

I hand the canister off to Lainey at the doorway to the front customer area, noticing a growing line. "I'll take care of the ice cream," I offer even though my feet are tired, my back is achy, and it's almost time for me to clock out. *Oh well.* I have another hour and a half before I have to pick my daughter up from school anyway. Might as well do something useful instead of rotating the washer full of sheets to the dryer or stopping by the store for groceries.

"Thank you." Such gratitude lingers in Lainey's eyes, easing the sting of sore muscles. With Kaylee out on maternity leave for her second child, and Becca out of town for her stepson's soccer tournament, we're stretched a little thin right now. The cupcakes in the kitchen that need to be frosted can wait for Jamie's shift tonight.

I take over the ice cream orders, filling several dishes, flavored cones, and chocolate-dipped waffle bowls. My most popular order today—and every day —is the confetti cone that has a distinct birthday cake flavor. Luckily, I made a massive batch of those cones before we realized how low on sprinkles we were running.

"What is *that*?" a deep, suave voice asks when I spin around with my most popular concoction. I'm stunned into silence by the owner of the voice. It's not just the motorcycle jacket or the tattoos peeking out beneath his sleeves. It's those dangerous ocean blue eyes. "Does it have a name?" he asks when I fail to answer.

"Birthday confetti explosion," Lainey answers for me, taking the cone and handing it to the customer in line. "You want one?"

"Yes."

I spin around toward the ice cream station quickly, desperate to break the trance those damn eyes have on me. The man has bad boy written over every inch of him. It doesn't matter that I've sworn off love, relationships, and even sex for the past several years. Bad boys are *still* my fucking weakness.

Despite the ever-growing line, it takes me twice as long to assemble a dessert I should be able to create in my sleep. My hands are shaky with nerves. I can feel those eyes penetrating my body from behind, sweeping over it.

When I was sixteen, I got pregnant with my daughter on prom night. The bad boy who thought it'd be hot to do it in the back seat of his Nova didn't think it was so hot that he knocked me up. He skipped town before Amelia was born. Outside of the child support check he remembers to send once or twice a year, I haven't heard or seen him since. My daughter has never met her biological father.

You think I'd have learned my lesson after him.

But no.

I *still* crave a bad boy. One who rides a motorcycle, is all tatted up, and can incinerate panties with one look. The man standing in front of counter is the epitome of kryptonite. *My* kryptonite. *Fuck!* I can feel the chemistry in the air like a thick, alluring fog.

If I asked him for a ride on his motorcycle, I think he'd give me one.

But I *don't* give into these impulses anymore. Amelia is my whole world, and letting my reckless side free promises nothing good for her.

"Here you go," I say, handing the cone over.

"Now that is a thing of beauty." But his eyes aren't on the cone. They're on me. "What's your name?" he asks.

Because we have other customers in line eavesdropping, telling him that my name is none of his damn business feels rude. Everyone in town knows who the Belmont sisters are. "Eliza."

"That's a beautiful name."

Despite my resolve not to get suckered into his charms, my nipples tingle at his words. It's been so long since a man has touched me in an intimate way. Longer still since I've enjoyed any of it. I dated some when Amelia was too young to ask questions, but the minute any of those men found out I was a single mother, they vanished.

Imagining this bad boy's hands on me makes me shiver...in a good, *dangerous* way.

"Thanks," I finally say.

"I'm Tucker, by the way. Tucker Ames."

Dammit, even his name sounds badass. "You new to town, Tucker?" Our town isn't a tiny dot on the map by any means, but I know I haven't seen him before. I doubt a man like him would frequent a bakery, and I'd remember if we passed in a grocery store aisle or crossed paths at a gas station.

"Moved here a couple of weeks ago," he admits. "Charming place."

Warning bells sound in my head, screaming at me to run the other way. He's not just some sexy badass who rides a motorcycle and has a few tattoos. I'd bet my ice cream recipe he's the kind of man who doesn't stay in one place for long. "Need anything else Tucker?" I ask as Lainey mouths another order to me.

"When you do get off, Eliza?"

If I was a free woman without a child, I might give him the answer he wants. But I'm a responsible single mother. "I don't. Have a nice day, Mr. Ames."

2

TUCKER

I steer my bike into the parking spot I've claimed as my own outside SPRINKLES ON TOP and kick out the kickstand. Considering that I've stopped at the bakery every day this week, no one would dare argue with me. I'm addicted to Eliza's smile, and this bakery is the only place in town I can get my fix.

Every day I've asked her out, and every day she's shot me down.

But each time I ask, I feel her resolve weakening. I can see the temptation warring in those pretty brown eyes. She *wants* to say yes. I just haven't figured out what's holding her back. And I'm not going to give up until I do.

With any other woman, I might've counted my

losses. I didn't move to this town to get tangled up with a woman—for fun or for anything longer. It's the last complication I need. I'm here for a fresh start —a better life than the one I was leading. I should be focused on slowing down and figuring out what comes next.

But every time I try to think about my options, Eliza's dazzling smile appears in my mind.

I've never been this hung up on a woman before.

When I first drove through the charming mountainside town, I didn't expect to stay long. A couple weeks, maybe a month. But now that I'm here, it's growing on me. It's far enough away from my past, and quiet enough that it shouldn't come looking for me. I can't deny that Eliza tempts me to put down some actual roots.

I should steer clear of her as I sort out my shit, but the hold she already has on me is too strong.

It's not just lustful attraction. It's something much more powerful.

It's fate.

Because it's more stalkerish to sit outside and stare at her through the window, I dismount my bike, remove my helmet, and head inside to sample a new flavor. With over twenty to try, I have a reason to keep coming back for a while. I've never been a man with a taste for sweets, but her ice cream is sinfully delicious. I can no more resist her creative, tasty treats than I can resist her smile.

"Tucker, you're back," Eliza says, flashing me that heart-stopping smile. Each day, the forced professionalism she layers on can't hide the truth. Our interactions excite her. I feel it. But why she fights it, I haven't quite figured out. "Just can't stay away, can you?"

"I'm addicted," I admit, winking.

The blush on her cheeks is unmistakable, despite her attempt to duck her head and hide it. "Which one do you want to try today?"

I lean against the counter, sneaking glances of those generous tits trapped beneath a silk blouse. Every night this week has been filled with lustful dreams of the two of us naked. I wonder if she'd run far away if I confessed I'd gotten myself off in the shower this morning thinking about her in the tight red top she wore yesterday—and nothing else. "That red velvet delight has been calling my name all day."

"One red velvet delight coming right up."

"Eliza, are there any more sprinkles?" A woman asks from the doorway leading into kitchen. Most of the women who work here are sisters—all but one if I'm keeping my facts straight. I've tried to remember all their names, partially to impress Eliza. Partially because I feel they hold a place in my future as well. I've never had a reliable family, but I've already fantasized about being a part of hers.

"No more sprinkles," she answers as she assembles my order. "Order on the way, though. He should be here within the hour."

"Bad news," another woman, a redhead, chimes in. *Hannah?* I'm almost certain that's her name. "Accident on the highway. Semi rolled over and is blocking all lanes of traffic."

"Oh no," Eliza groans. "Please tell me—"

"Pete's on the phone," Hannah adds. "Says he's stuck on the wrong side of it. Complete standstill. He's trapped without any way to turn around."

I stiffen at the mention of another man's name. It's completely irrational to be jealous of a man I've never met. I don't know who this *Pete* is to Eliza, but she looks absolutely crushed that he won't be making an appearance.

"But the big promotion tomorrow..." Eliza sucks in a breath so deep that her shoulders drop several inches when she lets it out. In a quieter tone she adds, "We can't afford to wait until morning. I could make a trip to the city after I pick up Amelia, but it'll be so late."

"I'll pick up Amelia," Hannah offers, leaving me to wonder who this girl is. It's the first time anyone has mentioned her in my presence.

"Who's Pete?" I ask, because the jealousy in me can't be tamed any other way. I already know what I'm going to offer, but I want to know what I'm getting into before I do. If I'll be escorting her to a lover, I might have to reconsider.

"Our delivery driver," the blonde—*Lainey?* —answers.

Relief floods me, settling my wildly beating heart and allowing me to relax the fingers I didn't even realize I was clenching into a fist. "I can get through stopped traffic. No problem."

Three pairs of eyes turn and look at me, several seconds passing before her two sisters crack smiles. Eliza's the first one to speak. "Could you really?"

"Just some sprinkles to pick up, right?" I have some storage space on the bike, but not much. I'll make it work for Eliza, whatever it takes.

"It's a small shipment," Eliza confirms.

"Got a helmet?"

"What?" Eliza's chocolatey eyes go wide. "I'm not —I mean, I can't go *with* you."

"You have to," Lainey says. "Pete can't just hand your mail over to someone else."

"I'll pick up Amelia," Hannah says again. "Go get our sprinkles. The success of tomorrow's promotion is depending on you."

After several minutes of avoiding my intense gaze, Eliza finally meets it with her own. My heart pounds in my chest at the thought of her pressed up behind me on the bike, the wind whipping around us as she holds on tight. "I have a helmet at home," Eliza admits. "Follow me there?"

"Gladly."

3

ELIZA

Riding on the back of Tucker's motorcycle is exhilarating. It takes all of two seconds to push out the worried mom in me and give way to the rebellious girl who used to love walking on the wild side. I may only have a chance to set her free on this short drive, but I'm soaking up every moment.

I wrap my arms tighter around Tucker's waist, but not because I'm afraid. It's so I can memorize the feel of my body pressed against his, inhaling the scent of leather that transports me back in time.

I love my daughter with all my heart, and I wouldn't change a single thing that brought her into this world. But sometimes I wish I could go back and visit a time before I had the added responsibility—

what I wouldn't give to enjoy just a few hours of that freedom.

"What's his truck look like?" Tucker asks at the last stoplight before the highway.

"White box van. Blue writing."

I asked Hannah to call Pete back to make sure he'd be okay with this pickup arrangement, but we didn't wait around long enough for her to give me the answer. I'm planning to beg if I have to.

"These sprinkles are pretty important to you?" Tucker asks.

"They'll make or break tomorrow." I don't have a chance to elaborate because the light turns to green. I tighten my grip and hang on as Tucker turns onto the highway. Within a mile, tail lights blink like a sky full of red stars.

Tucker weaves through the slowed and halted traffic like a man who's spent his entire life on a bike. The way he handles each move is incredibly hot.

I'm almost sorry I've shot him down so many times this week.

Almost.

But no matter how attracted I am to him—and let's be honest, I've had some *very* naughty dreams about Tucker and this bike—I can't give in. I can't bring a man into Amelia's life, especially one who isn't likely to stay in town for more than a few weeks before he moves onto the next thrill.

Maybe we could just have a little fun together... I

push out the tempting thought. Whatever lingers between Tucker and me is more than a little bit of lust that can be sated with a night or two of hot sex. I'd be a fool to think otherwise.

I spot Pete's truck ahead and point over Tucker's shoulder. He nods then shifts into a higher gear, forcing me to grab on with both hands again.

Pete's feet hang out the driver's side window, crossed at the ankles. When the motorcycle engine cuts out, I hear the distinct sound of snoring coming from inside the van. "Pete?" I holler, hoping to give him warning so I don't startle the poor man. "Pete, are you in there?"

He startles anyway, banging shins against the frame. A few cusses later, he finally sees me standing outside his window. "Eliza, what are you doing out here?"

I swallow down the dread so he can't see it on my face. "I thought Hannah called you."

Pete grabs his phone from his cupholder. "Guess I missed some calls," he mutters.

"I need a package," I say in my sweetest tone. "Any chance I can pick it up from you now?"

Pete startles again, this time with widening eyes, when he spots Tucker. "Who's this?"

"My ride." I answer because I can feel the friction in the air between the two men—Tucker's misplaced jealousy and Pete's overprotective big brother attitude. I almost tell Tucker that Pete is happily married with three kids, but I have to admit his jealousy turns me on.

"I'm not supposed to," Pete says pushing open the door of the van, "But since you came all this way."

"Thank you!"

"What's this promotion all about anyway?" Tucker asks, standing much closer than I realized as Pete walks around behind the van and opens the door. The scent of leather nearly blinds me with desire.

"It's called Sprinkles Palooza."

"Interesting name. Your idea?"

"Yeah. My first promotional idea. But without sprinkles—"

"Just need you to sign for it," Pete says, handing over the box. My eyes widen as I wonder how in the world we're going to make it fit on the bike. If I have to hold this all the way back, Tucker will be forced to drive ten miles an hour.

Tucker opens secret compartments on his bike. "Will it all fit if we take it out of the box?"

The urge to jump into this man's arms and kiss him hard on the mouth is overwhelming. I've been resisting him all week, and the reasons why are weakening by the second. "They're just in giant plastic bags." I hand over the box and let him rip it open.

"I'll pretend I didn't see that," Pete chuckles,

getting back in the van at the first promise of movement up ahead. "You two drive safe now."

"Thank you, Pete. I really appreciate this."

"We're all set, babe," Tucker says with that sinfully sexy wink.

I can't stop staring at his lips, no matter how hard I try to look away. Dammit, I really want to kiss this man. It's not just to feel those seductive lips pressed against my own, it's to thank him. At least, that's what I keep telling myself. I could thank his lips, his—

"Eliza, keep looking at me like that and—"

I don't let him finish his sentence before I pounce. I throw my arms around his neck and pull his face down to mine. Our lips collide, the want and desire we've both been feeling all week melting into the kiss. His arms wrap protectively around my body, making me feel safe and wanted for the first time in years. Our passionate make-out session in the middle of halted traffic earns us a few honks, causing us both to laugh.

"What was that for?" Tucker asks.

"For being so generous."

"That's all?" he teases as I reluctantly slide out of his arms.

"Don't push your luck." *Please...push your luck.*

4

TUCKER

I taste Eliza's kiss throughout the ride back to the bakery, unable to keep myself from fantasizing about where this night will lead now that she's finally let her guard down. I felt something in that kiss—I felt her freedom.

I want to make her feel that way every day.

Maybe for the rest of our lives.

I wait for the shock to hit. The urge to flee at a hundred and twenty miles per hour down the road and never look back. Because a thought like that has *never* crossed my mind about any woman before.

I'm not the settling down type. *But maybe I want to be.*

Back at the bakery, I let Eliza pile the different

bags of sprinkles in my cradled arms so she can unlock the door. "How many different varieties of sprinkles *are* there?" I ask so she doesn't notice how diligently I scan the area for threats.

"Dozens. Maybe hundreds. Different combinations for different occasions."

It's my natural instinct to take in my surroundings—to always watch my back after the life I led—but now I do it for Eliza's protection. If anyone tried to fuck with her, I'd beat them to a pulp.

Eliza waves me around the counter. "I need to put them in the back."

I wait until she's freed my arms of the bags before I pull her to me by the beltloops of her jeans and steal another kiss. The hunger from earlier emerges as our tongues mingle and bodies press together. Eliza moans into my mouth as my hands slide over her ass and squeeze.

"Stop," she pants. "Please?"

Though it's fucking hard to stop the animalistic side of me from taking over, I do as she asks and take a step back. I would never do anything she didn't want to do. I'm suddenly afraid I've got everything *very* wrong. "What's wrong?"

"I can't do this, Tucker." The desire in her eyes conflicts with her words.

"Why not?"

"Amelia."

That name again. Amelia is obviously someone very important to her. "Who is she?"

"My daughter. She's ten."

The admission shocks me, but not for long. In fact, it clears up the whole reason Eliza has kept me at arm's length all week long when the pull between us has been so fucking strong. "You don't think she'll approve of me?" I ask. "Is it the tattoos? I can cover those up—"

Eliza shakes her head. "It's not that. She's my world, Tucker."

"I admire you even fucking more for saying that."

She flashes me a smile, but it doesn't reach those pretty brown eyes. "I got knocked up when I was sixteen. Badass type. Skip-town type. Absent-father type." She lets out a heavy sigh filled with more emotions that I could ever hope to decipher. "Tonight has been...well, it's been a fucking blast. I haven't been on a motorcycle in ages. I haven't felt that alive in longer than I care to remember. Thank you for giving me that little taste of freedom."

"You're—"

"But it has to stop here."

I step closer, erasing the gap between us, and cup her face. "I have a past," I say honestly, locking our gazes, "but I want a fresh start. I want to lead a better, honest life. That's why I left. I would never do anything to put you or your daughter in harm's way. That, I promise you."

"I—I can't."

"Give me one night to change your mind," I barter, hoping she can't sense the desperation in my voice. But dammit, I'm not about to let Eliza slip out of my hands when I finally got a taste of the woman I've craved more than oxygen.

"My daughter—"

"I thought your sister picked her up today. Can she stay the night with her?"

"Hannah starts work at three in the morning."

"Then I'll drop you off at two-thirty." I lean closer until our lips are a feather's width apart. "Any more objections?"

"I'm in charge of the promotion tomorrow. I need sleep."

I look deep into those mesmerizing eyes, knowing what I'm risking by not looking away. Those pretty brown eyes of hers, I could get lost in them for all eternity. The connection between us runs so deep I feel like our souls are familiar. I can sense how badly she wants to say yes. "It's just one late night, babe." I plant a gentle kiss on her neck, followed by a nibble. She gasps. "Take a walk on the wild side tonight. I promise you won't regret it."

"Let me call my sister."

I press a soft, sensual kiss to her lips. A promise of what tonight will be all about—her. "I'll wait out front."

Tonight, I'm going to spend every minute we

have worshipping her body and bringing to heights of pleasure she's never known again and again. If all I have is one night to convince her that I'm worth the gamble, I want the memory burned into her mind.

"I need to be there by two or no dice," Eliza says, emerging from the back.

I meet her at the edge of the counter and drape my arm around her shoulder. "You'll be missing me by 2:01," I say with a wink.

5

ELIZA

If anyone else were leading me down a dark, creepy road in the middle of the night, I'd be terrified. But with my arms happily around Tucker again, my head resting against his back, I'm in heaven.

One night.

I can give myself permission to let go for one night, right?

He turns into a dark, tree-covered driveway with a steady winding hill. The younger version of myself would've never batted an eye, so I don't let the adult version worry about Tucker being a serial killer.

The tingles between my legs promise me he has nothing but good intentions where I'm concerned.

I gasp when I first see the massive log structure,

illuminated by various outdoors lights. "You live *here*?" It's not what I expected of a man I'd pegged as a drifter.

"Renting for now," Tucker admits, rolling to a stop and cutting the engine. "But I've been considering making an offer."

Money has never mattered to me so long as I had enough to comfortably take care of my daughter. But I have to admit, I'm a little fearful to ask how this man has so much of it. Does it have to do with his mysterious past?

"Come on, babe," he says, reaching out a hand. "The clock is ticking. I don't want to waste a minute."

All questions and worries flee the second the door is locked behind us. I don't even care what the inside of the house looks like. All that matters is that Tucker's hands are on my body. He backs me up against the front door and devours my mouth. I arch my back, begging him to touch my breasts.

"All in good time, babe," he whispers against my ear. Taking my hand, he leads me through the house and to the master bedroom.

It's the sight of the king-sized bed that brings out my insecurity. I haven't been with a man in years. The only pleasure I've experienced is pleasure I've given myself. I feel way out of my depth. My breathing grows labored as the edges of a panic attack threaten to take hold. *Calm the fuck down, Eliza. You're going to embarrass yourself.*

"Hey," he says softly, taking me into his arms and holding me close. "We don't have to do anything you don't want to." His words are kind; not an ounce of judgement in them.

"I'm sorry," I say. "It's so embarrassing..."

"Don't ever apologize for how you feel, babe. Not with me." He tenderly kisses my forehead. "Do you want me to take you home?"

"No."

He leads me to the bed, turning down the covers, and crawling in fully clothed. "We'll take things as slow as you want them." He pats the other side in invitation.

I'm still embarrassed and frustrated with myself, demanding my wild side return so I don't chicken out from the hottest one-night stand in my life. *One night.* I keep repeating it to myself, but my brain doesn't accept it.

One night, dammit.

I slip my shirt over my head and toss it away before I lose my nerve. I don't stop there. I keep removing clothes until I stand in only my panties and bra. The moonlight reveals every curve and perfectly imperfect detail.

"You're the most beautiful woman I've ever seen, Eliza. I mean that."

I crawl onto the bed, fully intending to climb on to top of him and remove those pesky jeans. But Tucker sits up, stopping me. "Tonight is all about you." He scoots back against the headboard, inviting me to sit between his legs, my back to his chest.

Tucker's lips and tongue tenderly roam my neck as his hands fondle my breasts through the stupid bra I should've ditched. I finally feel myself relax and melt against Tucker's hard, warm chest.

Fingertips skim my skin, moving south toward my panties. "Spread your legs for me, babe," he growls into my ear. "I want to play with that pussy."

I nearly have an orgasm at his dirty words.

Tucker slides his hand beneath my panties, his fingers on a mission. I've been wet since the moment I got on the back of his motorcycle today, and it's only gotten wetter down there. He growls his approval as his finger pleasures my swollen bud.

I lean my head against his shoulder and tilt my hips back, granting him better access. One finger turns to three as he saws his hand against my center. Fuck me this feels so good. I'm whimpering in seconds, the burning desire I've felt for this man, not just today but all week, bursting through the surface in an alarmingly short amount of time.

"That's it," he says as I start to cry out his name. "Come for me, Eliza. Come on my hand."

A wave of pleasure explodes inside me, causing my entire body to jerk forward. Tucker holds me tight against him until I come down from my high. "Holy shit," I gasp. "That was so fast it was almost embarrassing."

"Don't worry, babe. I still have time. I'm not done with you yet." Tucker slides down until he's lying on the bed, his head pointed at the edge. "I want you to sit on my face and let me lick that pussy while you watch."

I remove the last of my clothes and hover above Tucker's mouth. "Are you sure—"

"Get that pussy in my mouth. Then sit back and enjoy the show."

I do as he says, positioning my center above his mouth and leaning back so I can see his face. His tongue strokes slow paths along my pussy as he reaches one hand onto my boob, playing with my nipple. He holds me down by the hip with his other. Slowly I rock against the rhythm of his tongue.

I don't know what turns me on more. How good it feels to have Tucker's mouth there or *watching* Tucker lick me. It's a slow build this time, which I'm only crediting to his perfectly skilled tongue and the fact that I've already gotten the quick orgasm out of the way.

"Fuck, Tucker!" I dig my fingers into his skin as the pleasure builds.

The first orgasm took me so fast I didn't have time to prepare. But this one...I feel the building ecstasy like an oncoming tidal wave. Not only do I not *want* to stop it, I couldn't if I tried. "Holy shit," I cry out. "Tucker, I'm—I'm—" But the rest doesn't come out in distinguishable words. Just loud cries and moans as I'm annihilated by incredible sensations I've never experienced before.

"Was that good?" Tucker asks with a knowing, victorious laugh.

"I want you inside me." Another orgasm might make me spontaneously combust, but I don't care. I need to feel this man inside me before our one night is over. I *need* this memory of walking on the wild side to pull me through those hard nights.

"We're out of time, babe."

"What?"

Tucker pulls me to my feet, holding me because my legs are wobbly. "I want to bury myself inside you more than anything," he says with a seriousness that makes me shiver in a good way. "But if I do, there's no turning back—you'll be mine forever. I need you to give yourself—all of yourself—to me before we take that last step."

The impact of his words rattles me to the core. My heart yearns to surrender everything right now in this moment, but I know I can't. "Tucker, I—"

"It's okay, babe. I know."

6

TUCKER

Taking Eliza home last night was the hardest thing I've ever done. I wanted to keep her with me forever. I wanted to bury my cock deep in her channel and claim her as my own. But Eliza's life isn't as simple as mine. She can't walk away from her obligations, and I would never want her to.

But that doesn't mean I'm giving up.

Far from it.

"What flavor should I try today?" I give Eliza a wink and a dirty smile.

"Pumpkin party seems to be the popular one. It's only available until the sprinkles run out." Despite how chaotic it is in the bakery today—meaning her promotion is most definitely a success—she still makes time to serve me personally. I take it as a good sign.

"Sounds good to me." I lean against the counter, admiring the sway of her hips and the curve of her body. If I'm not careful, I'm going to get a hard on in front of a crowd. The image of her glorious body is forever etched into my mind.

"Here you go," she says, sliding the cup across the counter with both hands.

"How much?"

"On the house."

"I can't—"

She covers my hand with her own, our gazes fusing and heating. "You saved the day."

"When can I see you again?" I shouldn't press, but dammit, the air is so charged between us it's a miracle there's not an electrical storm happening inside the bakery.

She glances at her sister, some unspoken favor lingering between them. "Tomorrow night."

I nod, doing my damnedest to remain cool. I've always had my shit together, always known exactly what I wanted, and never let an ounce of desperation make my choices. But I'm desperate for Eliza. Desperate to make her mine. "I'll pick you up at eight," I say with a wink.

"Tucker?"

"Yes, babe?"

"I want to know."

I stiffen, not eager to talk about my past. But if that's what stands between the two of us creating a future together and a chance to meet her daughter, I'll tell her whatever she wants to know. "Okay."

"See you tomorrow." This time, Eliza winks at me first. I have to shuffle my way outside fast to keep my desire for her hidden from everyone else.

Tomorrow night. What the hell am I going to do until then?

7

ELIZA

Riding on the back of Tucker's motorcycle is officially my second favorite thing. The adrenaline rush and sense of freedom are wildly addicting. But my favorite thing, hands down, is kissing Tucker.

We're making out like horny teenagers the second the door is locked behind us.

I've been thinking about this since the moment he dropped me off the other night.

I've touched myself, wishing my hands were his.

Tonight, they will be.

"Tucker," I pant as my shirt is flung across the room. He palms my breasts through my bra, squeezing them in just the right way. I nearly forget my resolve. I want him, and I want him *bad*. But not until I know the whole truth.

I still can't commit to a future with any man, much less one with a dark past that might endanger my family. But I'm prepared to surrender myself to him anyway. If I have to belong to one man—even a man I can't build a future with—I want it to be Tucker.

"Tucker," I say again as he unzips my jeans. "We—we have to talk."

"Sorry," he says, though the mischievous twinkle in his eyes says otherwise. It's the bad boy in him I fucking love. It makes my pussy tingle with want. The last thing I want to do is have a conversation right now. I want this man to slide into home. But it needs to happen.

He scoops me into his arms and carries me to the couch. "Just give me the highlights?"

"Right." He lays me down, pulling my jeans the rest of the way down. "I worked for a high profile security company." He kisses the inside of my thighs, making it so damn hard to concentrate on his words. "I thought they were legit, but turns out they were fueled by dirty money." Tucker loses his shirt, revealing the washboard abs I suspected he was hiding.

"So you left?"

"Not right away." He unzips his jeans and pushes them down. His boxers do little to hide his desire for me. "I'm ashamed to say I stayed for the money longer than I should have. I had debts to pay. But that chapter of my life is over, and it won't follow me. I made sure of that."

A whisper of fear from the other night returns, and I wonder if this house was rented with that dirty money. "What did you do before that?"

Tucker sheds his boxers, and my eyes go wide. My pussy hasn't seen actions in years, and now I'm about to be split in half by that Hammer of Thor the man is wielding.

"Special Forces." He crawls onto the couch, hovering over me. "Any more questions?"

I have several, but for the life of me, I can't remember a single one. "Nope."

Tucker peels away my panties with agonizing leisure. "This is your last chance, Eliza. Once I'm inside you, I'm claiming you for my own. If another man touches you, I'll hurt him. Either this pussy is mine, or we stop now."

I drape one leg over the back of the couch and drop the other to the floor, widening myself in invitation. "This pussy is all yours. *Only* yours." Because I'm completely certain after tonight, I'll be ruined for any other man anyway.

Tucker lowers himself to my opening, pushing inside an inch at a time. I grip the edges of the couch as my walls expand to take him in.

"You're so fucking tight, Eliza. I fucking love it."

He pushes inside me halfway, then pulls out. Tucker repeats the motion until he's all the way in, driving me wild with desire. I haven't felt this complete...*ever*.

"Kiss me," I plead, desperate to taste his lips with him inside me.

Tucker hovers over me, devouring my mouth as he rocks in and out of my pussy. I rotate my hips to meet his gentle yet hungry thrusts. Each time our bodies join is its own special high. I came prepared to surrender myself to him, but now I know I can.

I let go of all my inhibitions and fears.

"Fuck me, Tucker," I pant. "You're amazing. Please don't ever stop."

His deep, low laugh is such a turn on. "I could fuck you forever, Eliza." He stares deep into my eyes. "For the rest of my life. I mean that."

His words hold too much gravity. I feel the edges of fear creeping in. To push them out, I grab his ass and demand he increase the pace. Our gentle bumps turn into ravenous slams. I could fall in love with this man if only I let myself. I *want* to, but I have more than myself to consider.

"Come inside me, Tucker. Please."

"Only if you come with me, babe."

"Deal."

Our pace goes from hungry to insatiable. I have to grip the couch to keep myself from falling off. My inner wild side is exhilarated at this rough, hungry sex. I feel the build again, another tidal wave. But this one is massive. This one might kill me.

I don't care.

"I'm coming!" I cry out, gripping the couch cushions so tightly I might rip them apart. My orgasm knocks into me so hard my fingertips tingle. Tucker pumps harder and faster until he explodes inside my channel.

With his seed in me, I feel forever changed.

I don't question whether or not I'm in love with Tucker Ames; I know I am.

I just have no fucking clue what I'm going to do about it.

8

***

TUCKER

The past few weeks with Eliza have been amazing. I don't get as many nights together as I'd like, but I'm happy to take what I can get right now. Someday soon, I hope to change that. If I had any doubts about sticking around town and planting roots here, they're gone. Eliza is my future.

There's only one piece of the puzzle left: meeting Amelia.

Eliza has talked so incessantly about her daughter that I feel like I know her already. If I'm being honest, I never gave much thought to having my own kids until I met Eliza. But now I want a whole sports team of little ones.

I arrive at the local park we agreed to meet at and look around, but I don't see any signs of Eliza or Amelia. I park my bike and scout out a bench. But before I can even get the kickstand down, my phone buzzes.

"Hey, babe." My heart feels fuller than I ever thought it could feel just at the prospect of hearing her sweet voice. I'm a goner for this woman. "You almost here?"

"I can't make it," Eliza says, a mixture of disappointment and strain in her voice. "I'm so sorry, Tucker. Amelia has the flu or some bug. She started throwing up early this morning. I'm still cleaning up, and I'm so damn exhausted."

"We can reschedule," I reassure her.

"This is a sign, Tucker. Don't you get it? These past few weeks have been fun. But my daughter needs me. She's the most important thing to me."

My stomach twists at her tone. I know what she's trying to do. No chance in hell I'm going to let her. "Stay put, babe. I'll be over to help." I end the call before she can launch into all the reasons why I shouldn't come.

I speed through town until I'm at her door. I knock, but there's no answer. I push the cracked door open a few more inches. "Eliza?" I call into the hallway. I see the edges of socks around the corner. The evidence all over the hallway floor promises she wasn't lying. At least one of them is sick, if not both.

"Go away," she pleads. "I don't want you to see me like this."

I find her on all fours, mopping up Amelia's mess with a rag and bucket of water. Bags hang under her eyes, her hair is tied up in a messy knot at the top of her head, and my poor angel looks exhausted.

The man I was before I met Eliza would never voluntarily clean up a mess like this. But I'm not that man anymore. I'm the man who's fallen madly in love with an angel and will do anything and every-thing in my power to take care of her and her daughter.

"Eliza, you poor thing." I kneel down beside her, cupping her jaw with my hand. "Where's Amelia?"

"Sleeping. Finally." She lets out a heavy, exhausted sigh. "You shouldn't be here, Tucker. This can't work between us."

"I love you."

A tear runs down her cheek at my admission. Not the reaction I was expecting. "I know. That's why this is so hard. I love you, too."

I pull her up by the hand. "C'mon."

"What? I have to clean—"

"You need sleep. I'll get everything cleaned up. We'll talk after you've had some rest." I lead her to her bedroom, tuck her beneath the sheets, and take care of cleaning up. Maybe this day didn't go the way either of us planned, but I want her to know that I'll be here even on the tough days.

If she still wants to call it quits after this, then I will bow out.

9

ELIZA

Panic clenches my chest when I wake up in my bed. *Where's Amelia? Why am I in bed? What time is it?* I throw the covers away and rush into the hallway. The scent of lemon fills the air. *Everything is clean...*

It's the sound of Amelia giggling that calms my erratically beating heart. I follow that music into the living room and freeze in the doorway.

Amelia is sitting on the edge of the couch, hunched over the coffee table with a crayon in her hand. Tucker is sitting beside her, coloring one too. She keeps looking over at his picture and giggling.

My heart warms to see her smile. The poor thing went through hell this morning.

"You're up!" Amelia announces, drawing Tucker's attention toward me too.

"What are you two up to in here?" I asked with a raised eyebrow. But my smile is impossible to contain. This sight...it's heaven. Though it's not the way I planned for them to meet, this picture-perfect moment is still everything I've ever wanted.

"Coloring contest," Tucker explains. "I'm getting whooped by your daughter. You failed to mention she's an artistic genius."

Amelia rolls her eyes playfully. "Tucker doesn't like to color in between the lines."

Tucker gives me a helpless shrug. "She's right. I'm too much a rebel for that."

I mouth *that's why I love you* to Tucker.

"Why don't you grab a shower?" he offers, adding one of those wicked winks that make my nipples tingle. "We ordered a pizza. Should be here in fifteen minutes."

Actual tears prick the corners of my eyes, but they're happy tears this time. I can't believe I was about to push this man out of my life for good. He now owns my heart *and* my soul. "Thank you."

I slip into the bedroom to find a change of clothes that doesn't smell like death. A gentle knock sounds behind me. I spin, expecting Amelia. But it's Tucker. "Hey," he says. "I hope you don't mind—"

"If I didn't smell like the plague, I'd kiss you right now."

Tucker closes the gap between us and pulls me against him, devouring my mouth without a second's hesitation. His hot hands heat up my entire body, making me forget I'm a mess. "I'll always kiss you, no matter what you smell like."

I laugh at that. "Remember you said those words."

"I love you, Eliza. And I already love your amazing daughter. I want you both in my life—forever. I'll let you take a shower, but I want an answer to one very important question first."

"What's that?" But my heartrate flies, already knowing what my answer will be.

"Will you marry me?"

"Of course, I'll marry you."

EPILOGUE
A YEAR AND A HALF LATER...

ELIZA

"We need more sprinkles," Hannah calls to me from the front.

"Are you sure?" I shake my head, certain I refilled the canisters of sprinkles up front just this morning. No way we've sold that much ice cream today. We sell considerably less ice cream on cool, gloomy days.

"Very sure," she hollers back. "Hurry up please!"

I abandon the mixing bowl and the new flavor I was attempting to create, sticking it in the freezer, and hurry to the storeroom to find more sprinkles. The last time we ran out, I ordered a mass shipment. We had so many boxes of sprinkles show up I had to store some of them at my house.

"You're taking too long," Hannah says in the doorway of the storeroom, watching me climb the stepstool.

I look back over my shoulder, sticking my tongue out at her just to get a rise. Hannah's arms are folded and she doesn't look amused. "You need to get laid."

"I'm good, thanks."

I grab the canister of sprinkles and hop off the stool. "That impatient scowl of yours says otherwise," I continue, refusing to give up the sprinkles despite her insistent yanking. "When's the last time you've gone on a date anyway?"

"I'm not having this conversation," Hannah mutters.

"Why not?"

"Because all you, Kaylee, and Becca do anymore is talk about sex. It's getting old."

"He's out there, Hannah," I say seriously. "The man that'll sweep you off your feet and give you the most amazing orgasms."

Hannah shakes her head. "For crying out loud..."

"You just need to put yourself out there."

"I work the world's weirdest hours. Dating doesn't fit into my schedule. Would you please get your cute ass up front before I wrestle you for those sprinkles? We have a *very* impatient customer out there."

I scurry up front, willing to drop the topic of Hannah's love life, *for now*. I rush to the ice cream station, then freeze. At the edge of the counter is the man who gives *me* the most amazing orgasms. *My husband.*

"Took you long enough," Tucker teases.

"You're my impatient customer?"

"Not me." He nods at our son, sleeping in his arms.

"He's one. And he's passed out."

"He fell asleep waiting," Tucker teases. "If you hurry, we might make it home before nap time is over. Amelia has a sleepover tonight so..." He gives me that wicked wink that makes my panties incinerate and leans closer, and in a low voice adds, "I really want to lick you."

Guess the new ice cream flavor can wait one more day. "Is that all?"

"It's only the beginning, Mrs. Ames."

HANNAH

RESCUED BY LOVE BOOK 4

1

_____

HANNAH

In the five years that our bakery, Sprinkles on Top, has been open, the alarm has *never* tripped. Not once. Figures the damn thing would go off during my early morning drive to work. I'm the early bird, always in at three a.m., so this is now *my* problem.

Fan-freaking-tastic. Just what I need.

Did I mention today is also my birthday?

I've already called the local police department—our alarm isn't one of those fancy kinds that actually *alerts* the authorities. Nope, it simply sends me a text message. My sisters and I have discussed upgrading our security system, but our sleepy town doesn't see many burglaries. And considering the alarm has *never* gone off...well, let's just say it wasn't a priority compared to marketing and fun new ingredients expenses.

Fingers trembling despite my vise grip on the steering wheel, I turn the last corner and head down the alley toward the back door of the bakery.

And am greeted by Nothing, with a capital *N*. No police car, that is. Really? I had twice the distance to cover as anyone from the police station. *Okay. Chill, Hannah.* It's an easy decision to make. With no police car in sight, I'm waiting in my locked car.

I inhale deeply, sweaty palms sliding on the steering wheel, and assess the area. The beam of my headlights isn't exposing any threats, but I'm not taking any chances either. How long have I been meaning to take some of those self-defense courses? Only forever, but life has been blissfully hectic since the day we opened our doors.

Now I'm wishing I'd made the time.

A string of new texts chooses that moment to light up my phone in an array of chimes. Not gonna lie. I scream like a little girl. Geesh I am *jumpy*.

Elyse: Happy Birthday!!!
Elyse: Don't forget I'm taking you to lunch when you get off ;)
Elyse: I'm going back to bed. Please don't respond until the sun comes up XOXO

The message from my night owl bestie makes me

smile. Elyse never rolls out of bed before nine, but she makes an exception, every year, on my birthday. She knows I'm not only awake, but working. No amount of convincing from her, or any of my sisters, to take the *sacred* day off has ever worked.

I'm a slight workaholic.

After what feels like hours but is likely only minutes—probably because I've been super jumpy at every little noise—I see the flash of red and blue lights illuminate the alleyway.

I'm torn between waiting in my car until the coast is clear or getting out to rip the police chief a new one for taking so damn long. My decision is made for me when he shines a flashlight right in my eyes.

Pushing open my door, I spring to my feet. "Do you *mind*?"

"Stay right there," a deep voice orders.

"Oh for crying out loud," I say, though I stay put. "I'm Hannah Belmont. I'm the one who called you out here."

"Did you say Hannah Belmont?" The voice doesn't sound as old and crusty as it should. In fact, the deep timbre of it sends shivers through my body that I can't blame on the chill in the air.

"Yes."

Finally, the damn flashlight beam drops from my face. "Will. Will Bradley."

My body freezes as my heart shifts into overdrive.

Will *Bradley?* It can't be. "Wh—what are you doing here?" Coherent words are a tongue-tangled challenge as my eyes adjust and the silhouette of a tall, broad shouldered man comes into focus. "Where's Gunderson?"

"Retired. I'm the new police chief."

"You're not" I laugh, cause I'm certain I've heard him wrong. *Elyse, why didn't you tell me?* Surely, my best friend in the whole world would've mentioned that her hot-as-sin older brother had moved back home. *And* taken over for a police chief I'd never heard retired. I've had a shameless crush on Will since Elyse and I were kids. *Ugh. So awkward.*

"I'm police chief now," he repeats, looking everywhere but at me. Like I'm invisible.

"I thought you were in Chicago, or some big flashy city."

"Baltimore."

"Yeah, that one." I totally knew it was Baltimore, but I don't need *him* to know how closely I've followed any details Elyse gave up over the years. "You moved?"

"Wanted a change of pace," he says, checking the alley for anything unusual. Finally, he goes to the back door and rattles the knob. "It's locked."

It takes me a moment to realize that's my cue to open the door. "Oh, right." My heart races wildly, like I'm fifteen again. Back then, the crush was intense but harmless. He's ten years older than me, but that little detail seems a lot less important now that we're both adults.

I unlock the door and step back, allowing Will to go inside. I wait in the doorway as he flips on the lights and looks around. It's impossible not to stare. The way the man fills out his uniform—my lips are moist before I realize I've licked them. If I thought I had it bad for him at fifteen, it's nothing compared to the yearning I'm feeling for him right now.

But there's still the teeny-tiny matter that Will is one of Elyse's older brothers. She and her siblings have a rule—they don't date any of their friends. The rule didn't seem like a big deal to me when Will was several states away. But now...I shake away the ridiculous thought. Even if that rule didn't exist, I have a hard time believing Will Bradley would give me a second glance. He's always treated me like a kid sister.

"All clear," Will says, meeting me at the doorway and forcing me to hop back into the alley as he takes one more look around. I'm afraid if I get too close, I might just pounce. I'd have a hard time explaining that—to Will *and* Elyse. "Might've been a raccoon."

"A raccoon?" I raise an eyebrow. "Five years and that alarm has never tripped once. Now you're telling me some determined raccoon managed to set it off?" *On my birthday.*

"It's my best guess," Will says with a shrug. "Can

I see the security footage?" he asks, pointing to the camera above the back door.

"Yeah, it's in my office."

"Your office?" Will repeats, following me inside. I swear I can feel the heat of his gaze tracking every step, but it's entirely possible that the attention I desire from him is all in my head.

"My sisters and I own this bakery." I unlock the office door and lead him inside, praying he can't hear how loudly my heart is thundering in my chest. In this tiny room, it's impossible not to graze his arm with my own. "I think you've been gone too long, Officer Bradley."

2

WILL

"Please, call me Will." It's impossible not to let my gaze rake over Hannah as she bends over the computer, logging in. The last time I saw her, she was in high school. A kid, just like my sister Elyse.

But there is nothing *kid* about her now.

She's all grown up and every bit woman, with the body of a goddess and curves for days.

"This is the security footage, *Will*," Hannah says, straightening up and backing against the wall in the cramped office space. I'm afraid I make her uncomfortable, being this close to her, which is the last thing I want to make her feel. "I need to get started on the donuts, but feel free to take your time."

"Wait. You normally come to work at three in the morning?"

"Yes."

I frown, not at all happy about her answer. I don't like the idea of Hannah parking in that dark alley day after day. Working homicide for the last several years has affected my view of the world. I don't trust most people. I only moved back to my hometown so I could slow down, and hopefully regain my faith in humanity.

Just because I blamed a raccoon for tripping the alarm doesn't mean that's my leading theory. I didn't want to cause Hannah unnecessary panic until I know if there's a greater threat. My gut tells me someone tried to break in. "Maybe I should swing by this week when you come in," I add. "To make sure you get inside safely."

"I've been working this shift for five years," Hannah says, eyeing her escape from the cramped room. But like me, she must realize there's no way to switch places without some physical contact. The air between us is charged in a way that promises danger should we touch. "Do you really think that's necessary?"

"It's just a precaution."

I step out of the office, allowing her to pass me and go into the kitchen. I find myself glancing at the massive ovens as her jacket brushes my arm, trying like hell to shake away the impulse to kiss her until we're both gasping for air. She's off limits. My siblings and I have a strict rule. One that's never been a problem for me since I haven't lived at home in years.

But suddenly, that rule seems like the stupidest thing I've ever agreed to.

"You're sure you're not just after my donuts?"

It takes a few seconds longer than is appropriate for me to realize she means *actual* donuts. "I do like a good donut," I admit with a chuckle. "But I promise my reasons are strictly related to your safety." Beyond my call of duty to serve and protect the citizens of this community, I feel a compulsion to keep Hannah safe from all harm.

"I'll be out here if you need me," Hannah says, effectively dismissing me.

I drop into the rolling chair and rewind the footage to a few minutes before the alarm tripped, but the camera angle is horrible. Whatever it was— man or creature—is impossible to see.

"Did you want some coffee?" Hannah offers, holding up a mug in offering. Damn, she looks positively radiant with her red hair pulled back in a ponytail. Those full lips curled into a smile, and that body...don't even get me started.

"That'd be great, thanks." Our fingers brush when she hands the cup over, making my dick lurch in my pants. Thankfully, it's hidden beneath the desk. "I need to go back to the beginning of the night," I explain.

"You couldn't find anything?"

"Camera angle is bad."

Hannah lets out a heavy sigh. "Not surprised. Guess we got what we paid for," she adds with a mumble. "Don't suppose you know how to adjust it?"

"I'll take care of it before I leave."

"Thanks, Will." With an appreciative smile, she spins on her heel and gets back to work preparing dozens of donuts.

I could spend all day in fascination, watching her work. But when she catches me staring, I clear my throat and return to the footage. The angle is so poor that I rewind twenty-four hours, to the very end of the tape on a loop.

Not surprising, I find the angle is different.

Someone *did* move it.

I spend the next hour going through footage, looking for any clues but coming up empty aside from one very obvious human shadow at 2:28 a.m. Not only do I plan to meet Hannah here in the mornings to see she gets inside safely, I now need to add their bakery to my regular surveillance list.

"Those donuts smell amazing," I say to Hannah, stepping back into the kitchen. It's easy to forget I'm on duty when I'm near her. Easy to forget that life can be so cruel. That radiant smile makes me believe moving home was the right decision. "Do you really make all these from scratch?"

"Is there any other way to make donuts?" Her smirk is dangerous. Break the rules kind of dangerous.

"I guess there's a reason your bakery has been so successful." I'm stalling, both on telling her what I've found and on leaving. I'm drawn to Hannah in a way I can't explain. Asking her out is on the verge of my lips, family rules be damned.

"Happy birthday, Hannah!" a chorus of voices erupt as the back door flies open and a mob of smiling women bearing balloons and gifts take over the kitchen.

"Birthday?" I catch Hannah's eye for the briefest moment, but it's enough to make my heart race.

"Good morning, officer," one of the women says with a friendly smile. "We're not...interrupting are we?" She looks back and forth between Hannah and me, an eyebrow raised in exaggerated suspicion.

"Alarm tripped," Hannah explains. "He was reviewing the footage. Turns out it was just a raccoon."

Whether Hannah is telling her sisters this for their own reassurance or hers, I don't correct her. It's time for me to go, but I'll definitely be back tomorrow. I need to be certain Hannah's safe. *That's all this is. My duty.* But the words I replay in my mind feel more like a lie trying to cover up a dangerous truth.

3

HANNAH

"Good morning," Will says, that deep timbre of his voice causing my nipples to tighten yet again. *Every morning...*

"The alarm hasn't tripped since Monday," I say with an amused shake of my head. I tried to tell him I didn't need him here, but truthfully, I'll miss him when he stops showing up. "Is this really necessary?"

"I told you what I saw on that footage," Will says, reminding me about the hooded shadow figure. It was definitely *not* a raccoon.

Will has shown up every day this week to ensure my safety, and I have to admit, I'm getting kind of used to it. We've established a routine—he walks me from my car to the back door, he goes inside first and calls the *all clear*, then he proceeds to review the camera footage from the night before while I start my first batches of donuts.

He's gone before my sisters show up.

It's easier that way.

Three out of the four are very happily married. I swear they walk around with heart bubbles over their heads all day. I know they want the same for Lainey and me, but I don't need them getting overly hopeful about something that can never be. If they caught wind that Will stops by *every* day, they'd make something out of it.

"All clear," Will calls from inside.

Despite the lustful fantasies that've plagued my dreams every night since I discovered he was back in town, having Will around in the mornings is comforting. I don't know if there's any other serious threat since the culprit hasn't returned, but it's nice having Will around. Just in case.

"You sure you're not just here for the donuts?" I tease as Will heads for the office.

He stops in the doorway, pointing a smoldering look right at me. "I'm here for you, Hannah. The donuts are a bonus."

My heart flip-flops in my chest, replaying his words over and over as I set up my work station. I know what I heard, but I'm certain I'm reading too much into it. Sure, we've flirted a little bit. Okay, more than *a little bit*. But nothing has come of it.

We're familiar.

As much as I want Will to see me as more than his kid sister's friend, I think I'm cursed forever.

"Any chance I could get some coffee?" Will asks.

"So demanding," I say with a wink. *Shit, did I just do that?* I turn around instantly to hide my mortified face. Flirting with words is one thing. Winking...he has to think I'm nuts. My wobbly hands pour—and spill—coffee on the stainless steel counter. I scramble to clean it up.

"Let me help you," Will says, standing much too close for someone who's supposed to be in my office reviewing camera footage.

"You don't have to do that." When I turn to look at him, our lips are so close. I could reach up on tiptoe and...

"I want to."

My gaze darts to his oh-so-kissable lips, dying to know how they'd feel against my own. I've wondered for years if there'd be sparks, but I've never been this close to finding out.

"Hannah," Will says, his tone a warning.

"Sorry." I step back and let out a sigh, returning to the coffee pot while Will mops up the mess I made. We work in strained silence. *Maybe I'm not imaging this tension between us.* There's an electrical charge in the air whenever we're in the same vicinity. It's been there every morning, growing stronger.

It reminds me of my birthday lunch with Elyse.

The one where I told her how I ran into Will, and she joking said, *Don't worry. I reminded him that my friends are off-limits. He won't bother you.* I laughed with her, but inside it made me die a little.

Dating hasn't been a priority for me since the bakery opened. I've thrown myself into the work I love. I've gone on a handful of disappointing first dates that have never turned into second dates. I thought I was being picky, but now I wonder if I've been subconsciously holding out for Will. *Totally ridiculous.*

"Can I have that?" Will asks, nodding at the mug of coffee I've wiped down and refilled. I've been clinging to it like some sort of pathetic lifeline.

I set the cup down and hold both my hands up. "I put down the weapon," I say, hoping he can't hear the shakiness in my voice. Even after all these years of not seeing him, I'm still just as nervous and giddy around him as I was a decade ago.

Will's deep laugh causes tingles between my legs.

"Any, uh, new threats?" I ask about the footage.

"Nothing yet." He should take a step back toward the office, but he doesn't move. His eyes darken, promising me that he sees me as a woman—a desirable one. I recognize desire when I see it thanks to my sisters and their devoted husbands. It's a look the men wear on a regular basis when their gazes land on their wives. "Hannah, there *is* a threat. It's a gut instinct, but I've learned to trust it. I've solved cold cases following my gut."

"What else does this instinct tell you?" Oh boy. Did *I* just take a step closer? My fingers long to play with the buttons on his uniform. Is he wearing a bulletproof vest or would my hand slide against his hard chest?

"Hannah." The warning this time comes out in a growl. I can't keep my eyes off his lips. More than once, I've caught his gaze dropping to my cleavage— which is the very reason I wore this low-cut shirt today.

"I used to have the biggest crush on you." The words escape as barely more than a whisper, but I know Will heard them. He sets his coffee down and take half a step closer.

"*Used* to?" he challenges.

I shouldn't do this. I should stop this game we're playing before something happens we can't take back. I'm not trying to come between my best friend and her brother. But maybe, just maybe, something *real* could happen between Will and me. Something long term. Surely Elyse will come around... "I think I'm way past *crush* now."

Will's lips descend on mine in one quick motion. I'm swept into his arms as our lips move together with hunger. My breasts smash against his chest as his hands sweep up and down my back. One settles on my ass and squeezes. My laugh turns into a moan as he squeezes again.

If I thought I wanted Will bad before, it's nothing compared to the desire coursing through me now. I *have* to have him.

The creak of the back door forces us to bolt apart. Will's halfway across the room before Lainey's head lifts from whatever she was stuffing in her purse. "Good morning," she says to both of us, her eyebrow drawn in suspicion.

"You're early," I say.

"Emergency cake request. Birthday party this afternoon and the mom forgot to order the cake." Lainey shrugs out of her coat as Will slips back into the office. "You know me, I can't say no."

Lainey's interruption is probably a sign to back the hell off when it comes to Will. But I've never been one to believe much in signs. I return to my sheets of donuts, sharing a secret, heated glance with Will that promises he doesn't believe in them either.

4

WILL

I'm a condemned man.

One kiss will *never* be enough when it comes to Hannah Belmont. Not when it feels like one *lifetime* won't be enough.

"You're distracted," Elyse says, her eyebrow raised in accusation from the opposite side of the booth. She's conned me into meeting her for a late breakfast at the end of my shift. "Don't tell me you're *already* hung up on a woman?"

I've been trying to figure out how to talk to Elyse since the first morning I encountered Hannah. I'm drawn to her in a way that makes no sense, but it's beyond gut instinct. It may as well be etched on my heart. But I've yet to find the right words to broach the subject. After that heated kiss this morning, I can't take *no* for an answer from Elyse. "Well—"

"Seriously, Will?" Elyse says. "You've been back in town all of two weeks."

Something tells me admitting I'm hung up on her best friend *won't* go well today. It's best to shut this down before it gets carried away. That conversation will have to wait for another day. "I'm not seeing anyone." *Not yet.* "Why did you really drag me out to breakfast?" I say, hoping to spin the conversation away from me.

"I can't ask my brother who hasn't lived at home in almost ten years to come to breakfast with me?" But Elyse won't look me in the eyes. Even without my extensive investigative training, I'd know something was up.

"What's going on, Elyse?"

"Can I at least order some pancakes before the interrogation starts?"

I let out a discreet sigh. "Sure."

Once the server has taken our order, I resume my intense stare. The one that usually gets criminals to fess up to serious crimes. Elyse, however, is a harder case to crack.

"Stop doing that."

"Doing what?"

She rolls her eyes. "You know *what*."

I let out a laugh that's been too rare these past several years. It feels good as hell to be home, which is crazy to me. When I left, I never thought I'd miss it. But each day I'm back, I'm finding more and more reasons to want to stay. To plant roots. *With Hannah.*

"What's the news?"

"I'm moving to Alaska."

"What?"

"Just for the summer."

I cross my arms and sit back in the booth. Elyse squirms as expected. "Why?"

"I need a change." There's more to this story than she's letting on, but considering I'll be asking her one helluva favor soon, I don't press. "I applied on a whim. I didn't think I'd get picked, but I did. I have to leave next week. You're the first person I told, so—"

"Wait, you haven't told Hannah?" The suspicious expression on her face warns me I should've been less hasty with that question, but now I have to roll with it. "She's your best friend, right? Unless that's changed since I've been gone."

"Of course it hasn't changed. Will, I don't know *how* to tell her. You can't say a word. To anyone. Not yet. Not until I figure out how to break the news to her."

This feels like a trap.

The domino effect of one tripped alarm earlier this week has created quite the predicament.

"Will!"

"I won't say anything," I finally say, and only

because she knows about the tripped alarm. What she doesn't know is that I've been meeting Hannah at the bakery every morning to ensure her safety. Elyse sure as hell can't find out about that steamy kiss this morning.

My phone buzzes just as our pancakes arrive. I discreetly check it under the table.

Hannah: I'm off in an hour.
Hannah: Do you want to pick up where we left off?

It's a battle to keep my breathing steady as my pulse triples. I should say no, or even just mention that I'm at breakfast with Elyse. That would be answer enough. But the buzz of her kiss still lingers on my lips. I'm desperate for more.

If Elyse really is leaving in a week...would it be so terrible to keep it a secret? Let her find out when she returns home? An entire summer *would* be long enough to prove that I'm serious about Hannah.

Will: Your place or mine?
Hannah: Mine.

"I thought you were off work?" Elyse says with an accusing raised eyebrow.

"I am."

"Then who are you texting?"

"Elyse, I'm the police chief. Just because I'm off

duty doesn't mean the crime waits for my next shift." I only feel a small tinge of guilt for the evasive response. "How are your pancakes?"

"I bet it's that girl."

"What girl?" There is nothing *girl* about Hannah Belmont. She is every bit a curvy goddess of a woman.

"Go ahead and play dumb," Elyse says. "I'll figure it out before I get on that plane."

"Good luck." I'm good at bluffing or otherwise my sister would see right through that. I still have no fucking clue how I'm going to navigate these murky waters with the two most important women in my life keeping secrets from each other, but I'm too far sucked in now to turn back.

5

HANNAH

My hands are still shaky from that daring text. One I sent because I flipped a quarter and it landed tails up. I'm shocked as hell that Will agreed so readily to come over. If I had known one coin toss was all it would take...

The knock on my door makes me squeak in surprise. How did an hour fly by so quickly?

I pause at the hallway mirror, double checking my makeup. The bakery kitchen has a way of melting some of my waterproof mascara that's supposed to outlast a shower. I don't want to scare the man off before I ever get him inside.

My hand is on the door knob when the fear hits

me. What if Elyse stops by today? She's supposed to be working an afternoon shift. But that's never stopped her from a surprise visit. A second knock on the door forces me to push away the worry and open the door.

I haven't had the pleasure of seeing Will in civilian clothes since his return. The man looks damn fine in a police uniform, but he looks delicious in those jeans and fitted T-shirt that shows off those muscles I knew he's been hiding.

"Hey."

"Hey yourself."

Will glances over his shoulder, then back at me. "Can I come in?"

It's now I notice his truck isn't in the driveway or even parked along the street in front of my house. I stretch my neck through the opening and spot it a block away. *He's worried about Elyse, too.*

"Hannah?"

"Oh, sorry!" I hop out of the way so he can hurry inside. I close the door and flip the deadbolt until it clicks into place. But I'm having the hardest freaking time turning around and facing the man I was lips-deep with this morning.

My heart races like a freight train on a mission.

"Hannah?" Will says, my name on his lips gentle with an edge of sensual.

Slowly I turn to face him, unable to control my

heavy breathing. His darkened eyes drop to my breasts, warning me he knows just how nervous I am. The damn things are rising and falling like I've just run a mile from a hungry bear.

"Hey there." My voice is two octaves too high and squeaky.

"Are you sure you want me here?" he asks.

I flatten my back against the front door as he takes a stride toward me. "Yes, I want you here."

Gently, he brushes knuckles against my cheek. "We don't have to do anything you don't want to." He takes another step closer, eliminating most of the space between us, and waits. As if he's testing the waters and giving me every opportunity to stop this from happening.

But I don't want to stop it.

I've dreamed about this for so long. Fantasized what it would be like to touch Will's bare chest, run my hands greedily along his neck, to wrap my hand around his cock and bring him to the utter heights of pleasure. I've spent so many nights with my hands on my myself, imagining they were *his* hands.

"I want this, Will," I finally say, his lips half a breath from my own. I snake my hand around his neck. "I want *you*."

Our lips collide in a hungry, heated passion. His strong arms ensnare me in a trap I never want to be free of. Our bodies mold together as our tongue dance. He tastes of coffee and syrup. I moan against his mouth, deepening the kiss.

I'm dizzy already. This kiss cements what I suspected this morning. I'm in love with Will Bradley. It's not just some crush or infatuation. I'm head over heels for the man. The sparks this passionate entanglement create could burn my house down, and I wouldn't care.

Hot hands slide beneath my black shirt, rolling the fabric up until it's off. "I could fuck you right here," Will says with a hungry growl against my ear as he slides his hand into the front of my leggings. "But I'd rather take you in your bed."

My body shivers in anticipation. The way the man says the word *fuck* turns me on in ways I can't begin to describe. Add that to the way his fingers are teasing my pussy through my panties...I've never felt so desired in all my life. "Upstairs," I breathlessly say. "Bed is upstairs."

When he kisses me this time, I can tell something has shifted. It's as if he's transferring deep emotions straight into my soul. "Everything is going to be different," he says, warning in his tone. "I can't have you just once, Hannah. If all I am to you is a good, one-time fuck—"

"You're not." I almost blurt that I love him, but I'm worried that might be a mood killer. "Once will never be enough for me either."

"Good answer."

This feels like the wrong time to mention the Elyse complication, so I don't. Instead, I lead Will to my bedroom so he can do the one thing I've wanted him to do for years—bury himself inside me and make me his.

6

WILL

The moment I made the decision to answer Hannah's text, I knew there was no turning back. I'm falling for her. She's like quicksand, and I don't want anyone to rescue me.

I follow her to the bedroom, gaze locked on those bountiful tits trapped in a white lace prison. She looks so damn beautiful, standing before me in her bra and a pair of leggings. Her red hair rests on her shoulders, making those eyes darker and dangerous somehow.

I slip off my shirt and zone in on Hannah. My fingers work the clasp of her bra until it falls to the floor.

"I've been dying to get a peek at these tits *all* week."

With a wicked smirk, Hannah lifts them with her hands. "What do you think?"

"I think I need to feel them pressed against me." I pull her tight against my chest, experiencing a new kind of euphoria with her skin against mine. My lips, never really feeling at peace until they're resting on her body, find her neck.

Hannah works at the zipper of my jeans until she's able to slip her hand inside. I groan when her fingers wrap around my cock.

"You're so big," she says with a gasp, her eyes wide. "I suspected, but—"

"It'll fit, babe. Don't you worry about that."

We shuffle toward the bed, losing the rest of our clothes in the process. Naked bodies entangled, we roll as our hands and mouths explore each other. Just the sensation of skin on skin is enough to make me come. But I'm saving my release for something special.

"Do you want me to use a condom?" I ask.

"You have one?" she asks, sounding surprised.

"I made sure I did when you booty called me over here."

"We better use one," she says. "I'm not on the pill right now. Don't exactly have a reason to be."

I'm relieved to hear that she's not sleeping around. I couldn't bear the thought of another man touching what's mine. Jealousy courses through me at the mere thought as I push off the bed and fish out the condom I tucked in my jeans pocket.

Hannah licks her lips, watching me as I roll the condom onto my cock. Her eyes darken. "Someday soon, I hope we won't have to use one of these," I tell her as I crawl back onto the bed. Someday soon, I plan to make her my wife. We won't need the pill or anything else because we'll be creating a family together.

But we still have a few hurdles to overcome before that happens.

Right now, I need to be inside the woman I'm falling madly in love with.

Hannah sits on her knees. "How do you want me?"

"Just like this, babe. Lean back on your hands." The sight of her tits stretching as she arches her back makes me crazy. "Spread those legs for me."

"Gladly."

I glide my cock through her wet folds, priming myself for entry. Hannah's delightful moans make me tease her clit a little longer with the head. "You like that, huh?"

"Yes!" She rocks her hips. "Can I do it?"

"You don't have to ask me twice."

Hannah reaches for my cock, using my shaft to pleasure herself. Fuck me, it's so damn sexy watching this. She whimpers, biting down on her bottom lip.

"Take yourself over the edge, babe. Come for me. I promise it won't be the last time I make you scream my name today."

It's a fight to hold myself back. It feels so fucking good in her wet folds. I could come, but I'm holding back. I need to release myself while I'm buried in that sweet channel. So I hold back as Hannah cries out my name and comes undone.

I take over, guiding my cock to her entrance. I push the head inside. "C'mere, babe." I sit on my knees, allowing her to ease on my length at her own pace. "Don't hold back, Hannah. I promise you're safe with me. I'll always protect you."

Our lips crash together as she sinks onto my cock. I let her control the pace to start, but within minutes we've rolled yet again. I want to fuck her in every position possible, but right now I want to be on top. I want to watch those beautiful eyes when I make her come this time.

The rhythm is hungry and urgent. I've never seen Hannah as more than my kid sister's friend until this week, but I feel like we've always been. Like we'll always be. I pump in and out, bodies slapping together, her fingernails digging into my shoulders, our tongues tangled together.

"Come for me, Hannah. I want to come together."

I wedge my hand between us, pleasuring her clit as I thrust faster. The sight of her tits bouncing with our motion is the final straw. I can't hold back anymore.

I flicker her swollen bud without mercy. "Hannah, come."

She cries out half a second before my release comes. I hold myself inside her channel, feeling more complete than I've ever felt before. A part of me I thought dormant and gone forever has been reawakened. "I need to come inside you without anything between us. Get on the pill, babe. Or we're making a baby."

"A baby?" At first her expression is shocked, but it gives way to excitement. She can fight that smile all she wants. I see the glimmer of happiness illuminating her eyes.

"I'm going to marry you, Hannah Belmont."

7

HANNAH

One perk I know I'm going to love is Will working primarily night shifts. He has no qualms when I beg for a nap. Falling asleep, wrapped in his arms, is the best feeling in the world. I don't know how we're going to make this work, but I have faith we'll find a way.

Otherwise, I'll die an old maid.

Elyse wouldn't want me to turn into *that*.

I don't know how many hours we sleep. Only that the sun has moved considerably since my eyes last fluttered open.

"Hey," Will says, a satisfied smirk on his face.

"Hey yourself."

He slides a hand up and down my side, making

my body tingle all over. All our clothes are scattered on the floor, but I don't think we're going to need them for a few hours yet. "I've been dreaming about you," he says as his finger wiggles over my clit.

"Have you?"

Will removes his finger, sucking my juices from it. "Dreaming about how you taste." He shimmies down beneath the covers before I realize what's happening. His tongue traces tender circles along my wet folds.

I spread my legs, granting him better access. I lift the blanket so I can watch him work his magic. I don't think I've ever seen a sexier sight than the one of this man between my legs, eating me out.

"Don't ever stop," I beg. "It feels so *good!*"

"I could eat you all day, and I just might." Will suckles my pussy, teasing and licking in all the right ways. He knows not only how to bring me to my knees, but how to give me lasting pleasure. I gently rock my hips to the rhythm of his mouth.

I catch him looking up at me and squeeze my boobs. Will moans against my clit in approval. The sight of him between my legs, my hands squeezing my breasts, and that expert mouth of his are too much. I wish I could ride this wave of pleasure all night long, but I feel the intensity building in my core. The urgency grows. I rock my hips faster, pinch my nipples, and gasp as Will wiggles that tongue against my swollen bud.

My orgasm hits me like a tidal wave. I call out his name, moaning so loudly I'm sure the neighbors can hear.

"You are so damn sexy when you come." Will slips out from beneath the covers, searching the room for his clothes. I'm slightly confused, because his cock looks ready for another round. He must catch me staring, because he says, "I only brought one condom, babe."

"One?"

"I was in a hurry to get over here." He slips on boxers. "Why don't we grab something to eat? I'll pick up a box on the way back. I'm off tonight."

I'm not, but I'll forfeit some sleep for more of that mind-blowing sex. "Sounds like a plan." I slip out of bed, collecting my clothes and dressing. I have to grab a new shirt because I lost my other one. *Darn.*

Will pins me against the door, pressing his lips to mine. I can taste myself on his kiss.

"Mind if I use your restroom?" he asks, nodding at the master bath.

I can't resist squeezing his dick through his boxers. Not my fault the man hasn't put on his pants yet. "I'll meet you downstairs."

I practically float down the stairs, feeling more alive and complete than I ever have before. I've always had a thing for Will, but this is something more. Now that we're both adults with healthy sexual appetites for each other, it's something else entirely.

He wants to make a baby.

I've always wanted children, and watching three of my sisters have babies has made me crave my own more than ever. But how am I going to convince Elyse that what Will and I have is worth breaking that annoying family rule they have?

Halfway to the kitchen, I hear a knock on the door.

My first reaction is panic. Did one of my sisters decide to stop by unannounced? The last thing I want is to explain why Will is here. Being caught by one of them is the surest way for Elyse to find out about us from someone else. She may not be happy about this new relationship at first, but she'll be livid if she has to find out via a rumor.

Hand on the deadbolt, I look over my shoulder to ensure the staircase is empty. Hopefully Will'll hear voices and decide to stay upstairs where it's safe.

"Hannah, you're alive!" Elyse announces, sarcasm dripping from her voice. "I've been calling you *all* afternoon."

Shit! Worse than I thought. "I was taking a nap." Not entirely a lie, just not the whole truth. "I thought you were working."

"You? You don't nap."

"Yes, I do."

"Since when?"

"Is something up?" I ask, avoiding her question with genuine concern. "No one's hurt, are they?"

"No, nothing's wrong. I got out of work early. Thought we could watch a movie or something."

I have zero excuses to say no to that idea, especially with Elyse on my doorstep. Zero excuses I can be honest about anyway. "Uh, sure." I discreetly glance back at the stairs; still empty. *Stay upstairs, Will. Please stay upstairs.* "Come on in."

"Did you know there's a shirt on your lampshade?" Elyse points out as I close the door behind her.

Double shit. "Huh. That's weird."

"Babe, are you ready to get—" Will freezes halfway down the stairs, his eyes growing to twice their size. Shit, this isn't going to be good.

"Did you just call her *babe?*"

"No," Will says automatically.

"And what were you doing upstairs?"

"Fixing a leaky faucet," I say, but the words come out as more of a question. Elyse doesn't miss that unfortunately.

Elyse yanks my shirt off the lampshade and chucks it at me so hard I barely catch it. "What the hell?" Her angry gaze bounces between Will and me. "Does our family rule mean *nothing* to you?" she barks at Will. "And *you,*" she says, turning her narrowed glare to me. "You're my best friend. How could you do this behind my back?"

"We were going to tell you," I say, knowing how stupid the words sound.

Will has slowly made his way down the stairs, approaching with caution. *Smart man.*

"I love her, Elyse."

My jaw drops open at his admission. "You do?"

Will looks at me. "Yes, I do."

I guess the baby talk was serious. My ovaries seem to do a leap of excitement at his confession. *Down girls.* "I love you, too." Maybe not the best time for this to come out, considering Elyse is furious right now.

"You two are unbelievable!" She stomps toward the door. "You couldn't just talk to me before you jumped in bed together? Secrets don't do anyone favors, you know."

"Do you want to tell Hannah *your* secret?" Will counters.

"What are you two talking about?" I say, looking back and forth between them, more confused than ever.

"Will, shut up," Elyse warns.

"What secret?"

"You tell her or I will," he says to his sister.

"What secret?" I repeat.

"I'm moving to Alaska."

"Excuse me?" My heart plummets to the floor,

imagining my bestie thousands of miles away. No more movie or wine dates. No more last minute pedicures or late night Chinese takeout. "When?"

"Next week."

I turn to Will, feeling a fire in my belly now. "You *knew*? You knew and didn't tell me?"

"See?" Elyse says. "This is why we have the family rule!"

I feel betrayed and guilty and mostly over-whelmed. "Everyone out."

"Hannah," both Will and Elyse say in unison.

"Out! I can't do this right now. I need you *both* to leave." I shove them out the door, lock the deadbolt, then slide to the floor.

What the hell just happened?

8

WILL

This past week has been miserable. Elyse won't talk to me. Hannah ignores my calls and texts. I've stopped by the bakery three times, but the second I'm through the door, she disappears from the front counter and hides in the back.

I've still kept an eye on her each morning as she gets to work, but I've been keeping my distance so she doesn't know.

I want to fix this.

I hate that the two women who mean the most to me are furious with me.

Two blocks from the bakery sitting at a stop sign, just shy of three a.m., my phone buzzes with a text. My heart leaps in hope, desperate to see Hannah's name on the screen. She's the only person outside of work who would text me at this hour.

But it's not Hannah.

It's an auto text from the Sprinkles on Top alarm system. Last week, I convinced Hannah to include me on any alerts until their system was upgraded.

I flip on my lights and race to the bakery.

I'm just in time to spot someone in a black hooded sweatshirt running from the back door. I abandon the patrol car and pursue him on foot. He's fast, but I'm faster. "Stop!" I yell. "Put your hands up!"

To my surprise, the kid cooperates right away. Slowly, he turns around. The glow of the streetlight reveals that he can't be more than twelve or thirteen years old. My heart squeezes. "What are you doing out this late?"

"Nothing."

There's the attitude I remember so well from my Baltimore days. "You might as well be honest with me. You're on camera now."

"No I'm not."

"So you're the one who's been messing with the camera, too?" I walk the kid back to the patrol car, deciding if cuffs will be necessary to send a message. I'm not going to arrest him, though I will call his parents. But I forget about the cuffs debate the second I spot Hannah, arms folded, leaning against the back door.

"Why have you been trying to break into the bakery?" I ask, loud enough for her to hear. If it's money the kid's after, there are half a dozen places in town that would be easier targets.

"For my mom."

"What do you mean?" Hannah asks.

"My mom's really sick. She loves your donuts, but we don't have a lot of money." I study the kid, eager to believe he's spinning a tale. But I remind myself that this is a much smaller town than Baltimore. Maybe the kid's telling the truth. I look to Hannah for her thoughts.

"You're Betsy's kid, aren't you?" Hannah asks him.

"Yeah. Please don't tell me mom." Tears stream down his cheeks now. "I wanted to surprise her."

Hannah sends me a look that confirms the kid's story.

I'm about to offer to buy the kid his donuts when Hannah jumps in. "Come inside. I'll get you some donuts to take home."

"Really?" the kid asks. "Why would you do that?"

"Because your mom is a very good person," Hannah says. "But you have to let Officer Bradley give you a ride home and promise never to try to break in again. We're upgrading our security system later today, and I guarantee you'll get in a whole lot more trouble if you try to."

"I won't," the kid says.

As much pain as I've suffered without Hannah

these past few days, my heart warms to life at her generous actions. Though falling in love with her was instant, all the reasons why are slowly falling into place. This is just another of many.

I have to fix this.

"Hannah," I plead. Our gazes lock, and I can see the love she feels for me in her eyes. But her lips are pursed in a thin, straight line that warns me she hasn't sorted everything out. Maybe it's Elyse's blessing she's after. If that's what it takes, I'm going to make it happen. Even if I have to break down my sister's door. She gets on a plane tomorrow, and I can't wait any longer.

I'll go after *nine a.m.*

9

HANNAH

Seeing Will earlier this morning unraveled my resolve to stay mad at him. Staying mad was the only way I was going to keep my distance until I worked everything out with Elyse. I don't know what to do now.

I'm still upset with my bestie too. The whole moving to Alaska thing really threw me for a loop. I'm happy for her and the adventure she feels like she needs to take, but I'm pissed that she kept it from me. Since I'm not exactly talking to Elyse, it's hard to get her blessing when it comes to Will.

"Hannah, can you please cover out front? We're swamped," my sister Eliza begs.

I've avoided the front counter most of this week

because Will seems to make a lot of appearances when I'm working out there. "Are you sure you need me?"

"I have to run to the school. Amelia's running a fever."

Dammit, I can't argue with her picking up a sick kid. "I'll cover."

"Thank you!"

I've barely tied on my apron when I see them. Will *and* Elyse. Neither one is smiling, but they're not scowling either. *An improvement.*

"Did you come for donuts?" I ask flatly.

"Is that what it'll take for you to talk to me?" Elyse asks.

"Yep."

"Then give me fifty."

My eyes go wide until I catch a glimpse of her smile. We've had fights off and on all our lives. We're never able to stay mad at each other for long. She breaks through my wall of anger and hurt, causing me to laugh.

"I'm sorry I didn't tell you about Alaska," Elyse says. "I didn't know *how* to tell you. I applied for this job and never thought in a million years that I'd get it. But I *did*. They wanted me to pack my bags and show up within a week. I leave tomorrow morning. I don't want to go if you're going to stay mad at me."

"I just don't understand *why*."

"I'll tell you everything over lunch." She glances

at Will. "Okay, dinner. You're going to be busy for lunch."

"What?"

"You and Will have my blessing. You have all of the Bradley siblings' blessings. The rule...let's just say it was created for a different reason. One that doesn't involve true love."

My gaze flickers to Will, recalling his confession of love.

"I want to know you're happy while I'm gone this summer. I couldn't imagine a better guy for you than my big brother. And I've already threatened him within an inch of his life if he ever hurts you."

I move around the corner and squeeze my bestie in a tight hug. "I'm going to miss you."

"I'm going to miss you, too. But right now, you have some making up to do." She squeezes me once more. "I'll pick you up for dinner tonight."

Elyse leaves me alone with Will. Oddly enough, there are no customers out front. I catch a glimpse of Eliza's guilty smile before she hides in the back again.

"I'm sorry—" Will and I both say at the same time, then we laugh.

"I love you, Hannah." He takes a stride closer, reaching for my hands. "More than I've ever loved anyone before or will again. You are it for me." Will brushes my cheek with his hand, drawing my lips closer to his. "Please, can we pick up where we left off?"

With Elyse's blessing and my insatiable desire to get this man naked, there's nothing holding me back. "Yes, I'd like that."

He sweeps me into his arms. The way I've missed him pours into our kiss. I'm filled with such powerful emotions. My entire world feels changed now that there's nothing standing in our way.

"Think you can sneak out of here early?"

I glance at Eliza lurking in the doorway. "I have a feeling someone owes me a favor."

"We can stop by the store. I'm all out of *protection*."

"No need," I say.

"You're on the pill now?" he asks, his voice low.

"Nope." I kiss him once more. "I kind of liked your other offer. The one about making a baby."

EPILOGUE
SIX MONTHS LATER...

HANNAH

"I can't believe you're still working," Lainey says to me as I waddle my way around the kitchen. She's working on a very meticulous birthday cake, so it's surprising that she looks up at me at all. "I don't know how any of you do it when you're pregnant."

"You know you're next."

Lainey lets out a laugh. "Yeah, right."

"She's right," Kaylee agrees, squeezing Lainey's shoulders when she sets down one frosting tube and reaches for another. "You're the only one left, so you can't outrun love anymore."

"You act like I've been avoiding it," Lainey says.

"Because you *have*," Kaylee says.

"What are you so afraid of?" I ask Lainey,

compassion in my tone. "Love is a very wonderful thing."

"For all of *you*," Lainey says. "You guys aren't me. You wouldn't understand."

"He's out there," Eliza chimes in. "I know it. You'll believe it soon enough. Once cupid sticks that arrow in your butt, there's nothing you can do about it."

"Hannah, your *husband* is out front," Becca calls from the doorway. "He's upset and wants to know why you're working."

"See?" Lainey says.

Hand on my lower back, I waddle to the doorway. I've always been a bit of a workaholic but I have to admit, I'm eager to get off my feet for the day. "I'll take off time when my daughter arrives. Until then, these donuts aren't going to make themselves."

I leave my sisters in the back to debate my words as I meet my husband out front. Damn if my heart doesn't race at the sight of him *every* time I see him. Some days, it still doesn't seem real that he picked me to be his wife.

"Hey," he says.

"Hey yourself."

"You look radiant." He kisses my forehead.

"Yeah right. I look like I swallowed a beach ball."

"I've never seen you look more beautiful, Hannah. I mean that." Will cups my cheek, drawing me in for a tender kiss. It takes seconds for the sweetness of that kiss to turn into hungry need. In seconds, my only priority is to clock out and get my husband home and naked.

"I love you, Will."

"I love you, too." He places his hand on my belly. "And our daughter. I can't wait to meet her."

LAINEY

RESCUED BY LOVE BOOK 5

1

LAINEY

"Lainey?" my sister Hannah calls from her office.

I swallow a growl, keeping my gaze focused on the carefully molded fondant. I'm putting the final touches on my latest specialty cake order and my sisters know better than to interrupt me at this stage. It must be important, or Hannah wouldn't risk my wrath. *Still.* "Just a sec."

"I have some bad news."

My hands freeze, hovered above the classic car shaped masterpiece for Anderson Auto's celebration. My first fear is that my best friend Celia is cancelling her rare visit. I haven't seen her since we opened Sprinkles on Top almost five years ago. "What is it?"

"Mark. He's got the flu."

Mark is our delivery driver. He's dependable, flexible, and he's never called in sick. Since we hired him a couple of years ago, I haven't had to deliver a single cake. "You're kidding."

Hannah holds the phone away from her ear, a disgusted expression on her face. "Nope, pretty sure he's telling the truth. Wanna talk to him?"

I shake my head, already calculating the lost minutes this delivery will cost me if I can't con one of my sisters into taking over the task. The only silver lining is that I've cleared my schedule for the remainder of the weekend to show Celia around. "Tell him to feel better."

Ignoring the constant chorus of voices, beeping ovens, and clattering pans that surround me, I zone in on the cake. I need to finish it. *Now.*

Picking up my half-full piping bag, I flick through the assortment of tiny fondant parts still waiting to be added. Only the front grillwork and the personalized license plate are left. Decorating cakes is a labor of love. I escape into designing them the way some people escape into books.

"Wow, that looks stunning!" Eliza says in passing, no doubt on her way to the storeroom for more sprinkles.

"Think it'll be classy enough?" No matter how many cakes I make, or how much praise they receive,

I get nervous each time a cake leaves the bakery. Today, that anxiousness is justified.

The Andersons are the richest family in town. A big corporate empire that feels out of place amongst the friendly small-town feel. Love them or hate them though, they have a lot of influence. Turning down their order would mean a bad rap for Sprinkles on Top—that's the power they hold over every small business in town. I'd never make a decision that would harm the bakery my sisters and I have worked so hard to build.

So, I put aside my pride and worked my ass off to create a cake fitting of their reputation—sleek, shiny, and meticulous. Stepping back from it now, I search for imperfections. I won't allow a single one.

Eliza touches my arm. "If they complain about that cake, each and every one of them needs their head examined."

"Don't suppose you want to be the lucky one to drop it off tonight?"

"Sorry, I can't. Amelia has a school concert."

As the day goes on, I find it's the same with the rest of my sisters. Everyone has somewhere else to be or another commitment. I'm the only one who has a delivery today.

I wrap up my day at the bakery and reluctantly load up the cake to make the prompt six p.m. delivery request.

"I don't have time for this," I mutter, pulling into a reserved parking spot for guests near the front door. Of course, it may just be the dread of entering this giant building. My sisters and I never had a ton of money growing up. Our family got by just fine, but we were taught to be happy with the simpler things.

Pushing the cart into the tallest building in town —we joke that the Anderson Auto corporate office is our mini skyscraper—I take a deep breath. *In and out. Ten minutes tops.* This building is a blatant flaunt of the Anderson empire. Everything about it is over the top, from the marble floors to the massive chandelier dangling from a crazy high ceiling.

"Just get it over with."

Delivering this cake for their office party celebration is the last thing tacked onto my very full list today. At least once this is done, I can go home and prepare for Celia's arrival. My sisters have been warned they won't hear from me before Monday morning. There will be lots of wine, dessert, and laughter this weekend. And maybe just a little more dessert.

I wheel the cart through the sliding glass doors, weaving my way through the vast area littered with leather chairs, and head toward the elevator. The lobby is deserted, as I was told it would be. Everyone is on the top floor waiting to celebrate some major milestone for the auto giant.

As I wait for the elevator to descend to the first floor, I catch a glimpse of someone entering the building. *Hurry up, elevator!* I'm not in the mood to chat with some stranger all the way up to the party.

The elevator dings, and I roll my cart inside. I let out a sigh of relief as the doors begin to close. It's not that I'm antisocial. I've just run out of patience for this week and I'm eager to start my weekend.

The very thought makes me smile like a fool. I can't remember the last time I *had* a weekend off. The word has lost its sparkly quality.

"Wait!" A hand reaches between the nearly closed doors, making me shriek. "Mind if I hitch a ride?" The deep timbre of his voice reaches my ears before I get a glimpse. The suit and tie I expect to see are missing. In jeans, a checkered button-up, and scruffy beard, this tall, broad-shouldered man looks lost.

"Wh—what floor?" I clear my throat, hoping to rid it of the nervous stammer I shouldn't have.

"Tenth."

"*You're* going to the party?" The words fall out before I can rein them back. They sound rude and judgmental. I never mean to come off that way, but my sisters keep me in the back for a reason. I rarely say more than three words to any customer not ordering one of my cakes.

"I am, unfortunately." The man leans closer, extending a hand. "I'm Mitch."

I stare at his hand for a few seconds and judge him yet again. *Much too rough for a place like this.* "Lainey," I say, lifting my hand towards his. When our fingers graze, my pulse triples. His touch is warm and...*dangerous.* Yes, very dangerous. The sooner this elevator ride is over, the better.

2

MITCH

I've been dreading this event all week, but Mother would've killed me if I missed it. As heir to the Anderson Auto Empire, she reminds me only every other day that my current lifestyle is only a stay of execution. My parents *allowing* me to work in a garage instead of at the corporate office is a favor. Nothing more.

At least I have a beautiful woman to keep me company for a couple of minutes before I'm inundated by reminders that the clock is ticking. That soon enough, I'll have to give up grease-stained clothes for a suit and tie. "What are you hiding under there, Lainey?" I ask with a nod at the stainless steel cover protecting a treasure on the cart.

"Cake." She clears her throat again, glancing at me and then away. "For the party."

"Sprinkles on Top?" I ask, trying to place why I've never seen her in the bakery before. I grab a dozen donuts or cookies for the guys at the shop at least once a week. I'd have remembered that soft blonde hair or her eyes, the color of melted chocolate.

"Yeah."

I glance above the door, watching the light move from number to number. *Four onto five.* "You're the legendary cake master," I say, remembering a buddy's wife bragging up a storm about her son's birthday cake recently.

"I don't know about legendary—"

The elevator rocks and jerks.

Lainey lunges for the cart, steadying it with both hands.

I reach for Lainey. My arms wrap protectively around her, my head tucking against hers. It's that or she'll crash hard into the cart. The scent of jasmine invades my senses as the elevator finally stops. The main light goes out and a flood light takes its place.

"Wh—what happened?" She's shaking in my arms, her knuckles white from her death grip on the cart.

"Elevator's stuck," I say with a half laugh. "This might be my fault," I add, slowly releasing my hold on her. The absence of her warmth makes me feel empty. I shove my hands into the front pockets of my jeans to keep from reaching out for her again and lean against the wall as my eyes adjust to the red hue.

"*Your* fault?" Lainey leans back against the wall opposite me, grabbing the railing. I'm unable to look away from the deep rise and fall of her tits brought on by her heavy breathing. "Do explain."

"I really don't want to go to this party," I admit. "I think the universe conspired in my favor." I don't add the bonus of being stuck in the elevator with a curvy goddess who's set my pulse to warp speed. I've been on a dating hiatus for several months, but maybe it's time to lift those restrictions.

"You couldn't have taken the stairs?"

"Have you heard of stairs getting stuck?"

Finally, her tense expression eases, her smile breaking through amid the red glow. "Are we just supposed to wait this out, or what?"

I've never been stuck in an elevator before, but I've seen movies. I know we're not supposed to jump up and down to make it move. Stuck between the seventh and eighth floor, that drop wouldn't be pleasant. I search the panel for a call button and instead find a closed panel with an emergency phone.

I feel Lainey's eyes on me throughout my brief

conversation with the security company. "We have to sit tight for a while," I tell her, hanging up the phone. "Someone cut through a power line in the ground. East side of town is out of power."

"What?" She pushes off the wall. The panic in her widening eyes is unexpected.

"Do you have somewhere—"

"We can't be stuck," Lainey says, shaking her head. She starts to pace in her cramped corner. "We can't be stuck." She looks at me. "Call again. You must know one of the Andersons. Surely one of them can get this fixed in two minutes flat."

She doesn't recognize me. Good.

I give a light laugh, hoping to ease her worries. It doesn't work. "They'll get the power fixed soon," I reassure, though I know it might be a stretch to hope for that on a Friday night. I have no doubt Mother has already made a call of her own. She doesn't care for her special occasions being interrupted. "We just have to wait it out."

"No. I can't be stuck. You don't understand. I need to get out." Lainey jabs at the button to open the door. "Open. C'mon, open!"

Though my elevator safety knowledge is limited, I'm pretty certain the most important thing to do if stuck is to remain calm. Lainey looks on the verge of a panic attack. A pinball set in motion, unable to stop from bouncing all over the elevator.

I do the only thing I can think of to calm her.

Stepping into her path, she collides with my chest. I swiftly cup both her cheeks and kiss her hard on the mouth.

3

LAINEY

I'm too stunned by the kiss to react at first, but within seconds my traitorous body responds. I melt into Mitch's arms as my lips move against his. His beard tickles my cheek. He smells like sandalwood and hard work. He feels like warmth and protection. The panic that threatened to unravel me dissipates, replaced by a new one.

I'm kissing a stranger.

The rational side of my brain kicks in. I push off Mitch's chest and back up into my corner. "What was that for?" The words come out as some strangled bark. My nerves are way too ignited with sensation for what just happened.

"You needed to calm down."

"So you *kissed* me?" The worst part is that I want to kiss him again. It's been so long since a man has touched me in an intimate way, and *never* has a single kiss awoken me like this. I blame it on the dry spell. All my sisters are married with families. They've been warning me I'll be next. But love has never done me any favors in the past.

I've done everything to keep busy and avoid it.

Yet, now that I'm trapped in an elevator with a stranger, I have a peculiar inkling to give it a try.

"I didn't have a lot of options," Mitch says, his smirk all too evident in the red glow. It makes him look even sexier. "You have a hot date you're gonna miss?" he asks.

I let out a *yeah right* laugh. "My best friend is coming to town. Haven't seen her in years." Maybe it would've been fun to see if he was jealous, but I've never been the type to play games.

"Her," Mitch repeats the word, nodding in understanding. "Maybe you should let her know you're...stuck."

I'm less upset about the kiss by the second. I can't imagine what the other alternatives were for getting me to stop panicking, but none of the ideas I conjure are pleasant. "Good idea." I dig my phone out of my purse, not surprised by the text announcing she's an hour away. Not twenty minutes old.

"Everything okay?" Mitch asks.

"Yep." I type out a text, letting Celia know I might

not be home when she arrives and giving up the spare key hiding spot. I mention elevator troubles, but not the hottie who's stuck with me. If she and I can just keep this between us...well, so much the better. "She's still on her way," I add, though I'm not sure why. I doubt Mitch cares.

"How long have you been friends?"

Certain Mitch is only trying to pass the time, I decide being honest with a stranger isn't so bad in this case. "Since freshman year of college. We both decided to leave to start culinary school together."

"So, you can cook *and* bake."

I give a light shrug. "When I want to." My legs are tired from standing, but I'm afraid to sit.

Mitch catches me staring at the floor. "Go slow. I think it's fine."

"What are you, an elevator tech?" I ask with a laugh, easing down to the ground. It's a bad day for wearing a dress.

"Just a plain ol' auto mechanic."

His appearance makes a lot of sense now. The jeans with a smear of grease on the knee, the casual shirt and work boots. I almost make a comment about the corporate crowd inviting their blue-collar workers, but I catch my tongue this time. "How long have you done that?" I ask, trying to sound casual though I really want to know about him. "Worked on cars?"

"Since I was old enough to hold a wrench."

"You love it then?"

"It's my calling, you know?" he says, sliding down to the floor. His legs stretch out halfway across the elevator. The tips of his boots rest an inch from my ankles. This seating arrangement shouldn't feel so... intimate. But it does.

"That's how I feel about cakes," I say, desperate to keep the conversation flowing and myself sane. It's the only hope I have of keeping my thoughts off of kissing Mitch again. Of doing other things with Mitch. Things I haven't done in far too long with any man. "I love getting lost in the creation process. My sisters know not to disturb me while I'm in the zone."

"Look at us," says Mitch, purposely bumping my shin with the tip of his boot. "Just two strangers in an elevator, doing what they love. Maybe one of us will get to continue living that dream."

Before I can ask him to explain those mysterious words, my phone chimes.

Celia: I'm early!
Celia: Found the key & started on a bottle of wine. Long drive.
Celia: Still stuck?
Lainey: Yep. Power outage. Could be a while.

"It's Celia," I explain, putting the phone away. "She's early."

"Here I thought you made your friend up to hide a secret boyfriend," Mitch says.

"I don't have a boyfriend, secret or otherwise." The red glow no doubt hides the blush I can feel spreading. If I were a fish, I'd have bitten the hook on the first glimpse. "I stay very busy with my business. I have orders booked solid for the next six weeks. There isn't time for much else." Now I'm rambling. Great.

"There's always time for something else. You just have to make it a priority," Mitch says, sliding around the corner until he's sitting along the same wall. He leaves enough space between us for another person. That I wish he'd slide over the rest of the way is exactly why this man is trouble.

I can't resist him.

I don't *want* to resist him.

For once, I want to forget about all my responsibilities and my sour experiences with dating. I want to give in to something a little crazy and thrilling. Making out with a man I just met while we're trapped in an elevator seems to fit that description to a tee.

"Lainey?"

"Hmm?"

"If you keep looking at my lips like that, I'm going to have trouble behaving myself."

4

MITCH

"I'm not staring at your lips," Lainey says. "Did you think I was staring at your lips?"

Her rebuttal is fucking adorable and the very reason I know things are about to get carried away if this power doesn't get restored ASAP. I'm tempted to place another call and name drop, but I have to admit, it's kind of nice that Lainey doesn't know who I am.

Women are usually more interested in my wallet than me. I don't want her to know I'm George Anderson's son. Or that I'm supposed to take over the entire company when he decides to step down. I'm James to my Mother and most of the suit and tie colleagues in this building. But I'm Mitch to my friends.

"You *were* staring at my lips," I say, biting down on the bottom one slightly to prove my point. "It's okay, Lainey. I don't mind. I want to kiss you again." Maybe speaking the bold words is the surest way to mess this whole thing up. But I can't stop myself. It's true. That first kiss sent sparks flying. I want to see if a second does the same.

"I—I can't get involved."

I scoot an inch closer. "Why not?"

"My schedule," she says, as if I should already know the answer.

"You *only* work?"

"No. But most of my free time is spent with my sisters and their families."

I scoot another inch closer. Heaven help me. I can *feel* the heat rolling off her. "What do you do for *you*?" I ask.

"Believe it or not, creating custom cakes *is* what I do for me. It's my passion. My escape from reality." The words lack the conviction I know she wants me to hear. She clears her throat, lifting her chin as if in defiance, but it only brings our mouths closer together. "I love what I do."

"But?" I rest my hand in the space between us, my pinky a feather's width from her own.

Lainey lets out a heavy sigh, her gaze fixated on our

nearly touching hands. The heat swirling in the small space between us undeniable, even in this chilly elevator. "I guess somewhere along the way, some of the fun *did* get sucked out of it. I used to have time to create custom cakes for the display case. Now I'm lucky to put out a couple sheet cakes a day in between all the custom orders. I miss that creative freedom. Making something on a whim and not having to worry if it'd sell."

I cover my hand with hers, giving her several moments to pull away. "What do you do to unwind, Lainey?"

"What's that?" she asks with a laugh, and her gaze lands on my lips again.

The woman is tempting me in all the ways she shouldn't. Fantasies of getting her naked, of tasting that sweet pussy, and suckling those nipples have been on replay since that kiss. I want to pleasure this woman in ways she's never experienced before, and I want to do it...*forever*.

I gulp a swallow, pushing out that last thought. It won't serve me to unravel where it came from or what it might mean. "I can show you," I say, leaning in and staring blatantly at her lips.

"What if the elevator starts working again?"

"The lights'll flip on before the door opens." I lean the rest of the way, capturing her lips again. Devouring her mouth and begging entry with my tongue. My hand cradles her cheek, pulling her closer. Her delicate fingers curl around the back of my neck.

I feel like a giddy fifteen-year-old boy kissing his crush. I also feel like any hot-blooded man ready to claim what's mine.

Lainey moans into my mouth as my hand drops onto her thigh. I yearn to slide it under the dress that's been torturing me since the moment I saw her in it, but I don't want to push her unless that's what she wants. "You have to tell me to stop if I go too far," I whisper against her ear.

Our gazes fuse, unsettling me to my very core. A connection lingers there, stronger than anything I've ever known. But most importantly, I see the trust she's extending me. I'll never do anything to jeopardize that.

"Keep going," she pleads.

Slowly, I slide my hand beneath her dress. I inch my way to her core, eager to feel that wet pussy. She spreads her legs for me, allowing my fingers to graze her silk panties. "So wet, Lainey," I growl against her neck.

"It's...been a while."

Selfishly, I'm glad to hear that. The thought of another man touching her pussy makes me violently angry. "I can fix that," I say instead. I hook a finger inside her panties and pull them over. Her back arches when I make contact with her swollen bud.

I kiss my way down the vee of her dress, yearning

to free those tits. But if I know my mother, she's raising all kinds of hell to get the power restored. I don't want to leave Lainey in too compromising a position should the elevator suddenly start to work.

With slow circles, I explore her wet folds. Her fingers dig into my shoulder each time I flicker her clit. I yearn to taste her, but I know the chance'll come later. Still stroking her, I slip one finger into her channel.

"Oh, Mitch!" she gasps in a raspy whisper.

Our lips join again as I fuck her with my hand, slipping a second finger inside. Her expressions and whimpers are so fucking sexy. Should that elevator door pop open, I'll be the one with something to hide. My dick is hard and aching to be inside her.

But Lainey feels special. More special than fucking her for the first time in an elevator.

"Gotta keep quiet," I warn against her ear. "Someone might be able to hear you."

She bites down on her bottom lip, strangling the moans to a low volume only I can hear. I keep going until I feel her pussy clench my fingers. I hold my hand against her as she shudders. Nails dig hard into my shoulder as she tries so hard not to cry out.

"Hope that helped you unwind."

Lainey rests her head against the wall, a satisfied smile spread on her lips. "You could say that."

It might be seconds or minutes later, but the overhead light switches on, bathing the elevator in normal light. We both hop to our feet as the elevator rises. I watch Lainey straighten her dress, smiling at the flush on her cheeks. "I want to see you again, Lainey."

The door opens before she can answer.

No surprise, Mother is standing *right* there.

"Oh good! You made it James." She strangles me in a hug, as if I've been lost at sea instead of stuck in an elevator. "We've been waiting for you."

"James." I hear that faintly whispered name and spin toward Lainey. The smile from moments ago is gone as realization dawns in those pretty brown eyes. "You're James *Mitchell* Anderson."

"You must be from the bakery," Mother says before I can get a word in. "Is that cake all right? It didn't melt or anything?"

Lainey lifts the lid with shaky hands, revealing a classic car. Though it's a quick glimpse, the cake is meticulously detailed. It looks just like Dad's favorite '71 Chevelle. "Where would you like it?"

"Follow me."

Lainey refuses to look at me now that the truth is out. I was worried dollar signs would flash in her eyes, not fury. *Shit*. Now what do I do?

5

LAINEY

I'm such an idiot.

I can't believe I didn't piece things together in the elevator. How did I *not* know that Mitch was the son of the wealthiest man in town?

"Here, you look like you need this," Celia says, handing me another glass of wine. The second the cake was moved onto its designated table, I ran for the stairwell. I'll have to go back for my cart another day. I wasn't taking another chance on the elevator.

It feels so damn good to be home.

Yet, it also feels empty somehow.

"I'm so glad you're in town," I say to Celia, forcing away thoughts of Mitch so I can focus on what really matters—my best friend staying the weekend with me. She has some big news to share, but wouldn't give me so much as a hint over the phone. "I've missed you."

"I've missed you, too."

"What's the surprise?" I ask, desperate to replace all memories of Mitch with anything else. If my pussy wasn't still tingling from his magic fingers, it might be easier.

Celia takes a slow sip of wine, her smile growing with each passing second.

"Celia!"

She looks ready to burst and, within seconds, does. "My sisters and I are going to run a B&B together! At first, I was just as skeptical as the rest of them. But we've talked everything over, and I'm so excited."

"Really?"

"Our great aunt passed away and left it to us in her will."

I take another generous sip of wine, willing the visions of Mitch to float away. Tonight is about my best friend and celebrating her life-altering news. "Where at?"

"Daisy Hills. It's a small, mountain-side town."

"You're leaving the big city?"

Celia nods. "I am."

Because it occurs to me this news deserves a breath-stealing hug, I set down my glass and wrap her in a tight hug. "I'm so happy for you."

"Grand opening is still a few months away, but I'm moving out there now to help oversee some upgrades. Namely the kitchen. You know how picky I am about my kitchen." Celia empties her glass of wine and pours another. We move from the kitchen island to my couch, and I bring the chocolate.

"How was your drive?" I ask, popping a chocolate in my mouth.

"My turn to ask the questions," Celia says. "What's with the flushed look? If I didn't know better, I'd say you got laid."

My cheeks heat instantly, both with guilt and a burning desire for a repeat. "It's nothing."

"Liar."

It's no use. Celia knows when I'm lying better than any of my sisters. She should. She was the one pouring the wine and offering Kleenex when Jackass Number One broke my heart in college. Jackass Number Two had been equally devastating in culinary school. I'd nearly flunked molded chocolate over him.

I clear my throat and reach for another chocolate. "I got stuck in an elevator. With a man."

"I'm going to need more wine for this story." She scoots off the couch to grab the bottle. "Start talking."

I tell her everything. The best thing about Celia is that she's never judged me for anything. She's as accepting as they come. Better yet, she isn't trying to convince me that my Prince Charming is out there like all my sisters.

"Are you going to see him again?"

"No."

"Because he has money?"

"Because he lied about who he was."

"I don't think he lied," Celia points out. "I think he omitted certain details with a stranger."

"Important details."

Celia waves away my objections. "Honey, that man gave you one helluva orgasm with only his hand. Imagine what else he's capable of doing. I'm not suggesting you marry the guy. But you deserve to have a little fun."

"We didn't exactly exchange numbers," I say, as if that'll stop Celia from pushing. But I know my bestie better than that.

"He works in a garage. How hard can that be to find?" She catches me with my mouth full of chocolate and caramel. It's a completely unfair advantage. I can't even grunt an objection to her scheme. "Drink up. Tonight, you and I are going to catch up on everything. Tomorrow, we're hunting down your elevator man."

6

MITCH

I haven't been able to get Lainey out of my head since she ran off last night. Mother dragged me around the party, practically shackling me to her arm so I couldn't make an early escape. By the time I left, Sprinkles on Top was closed.

I'm still shocked as hell that having money is a turnoff to Lainey. It makes me even more certain that she's the one for me. I know it's crazy to think like that about a woman I only met a day ago. But the reoccurring thought that she's meant to be mine won't go away.

Every minute I'm without her feels like torture. I've never experienced anything like it before. In fact, I was starting to think I'd be single the rest of my life because I didn't feel anything for any of the women I dated.

Lainey has awakened my soul.

"Is Lainey working today?" I ask the woman behind the counter. There's a vague familiarity about her. I assume she's one of the Belmont sisters, but I can't place which one.

"She's off for the weekend."

Of course, the best friend. I should leave well enough alone. Count my losses at least until Monday. But I can't shake her. Even if I can't see her until her friend leaves town, I need to hear her voice. I need to make things right. "If I needed to get a hold of her, what would I do?" I ask, hoping against hope that her sister is on my side even though she has no reason to be.

"Are you...are you dating Lainey?"

"Trying to."

"I'm Kaylee. I'm one of her sisters."

"I'm Mitch—"

"Mitch Anderson. You're the mechanic who fixed my flat tire a few years ago when I was stranded at Nic's house."

"You're Nic's wife?"

"Sure am." She yanks a strip of paper from the register and scribbles something on it. "Will Lainey be mad if I give you her number?"

"Probably."

Mischief twinkles in Kaylee's eyes. "Then I'm

doing the right thing." She slides the paper across the counter. "She deserves someone good, Mitch. She doesn't believe there's someone out there for her. I hope you prove her wrong."

"I plan on it."

I leave the bakery with a cheeky grin on my face, not giving two fucks who looks at me like I've lost my mind. Two blocks from the bakery, I pull into a mostly empty parking lot and dial her number. I'm about to admit defeat after the fourth ring when she answers.

"Who is this?"

"Have dinner with me." I'm afraid if I say my name, she'll hang up on me instantly. This tactic might buy me another minute or two.

"Dinner? I don't even know you."

"Oh, but you do."

"Mitch?"

"Have dinner with me, Lainey," I say again, pleading this time. "Give me a chance to make everything right between us."

"No."

"Why not?"

"My best friend is in—"

"This is the best friend," another woman says over the phone. "Lainey's going out with you tonight. Pick her up at seven. She'll text you the address."

"Seven it is." I end the call with a smug smile. For once, it feels like everything is falling into place. I'm going to do everything I can think of to make this evening as romantic as possible. I don't know why Lainey feels like she can't find true happiness. But I'm going to show her that she not only can, but that she deserves only the best.

7

LAINEY

"I hope this is okay," Mitch says as we park in his driveway. My eyes are still locked on the massive cabin-style home. Everything about it is elegant and over the top. It feels several leagues away from my own lifestyle.

"It's fine."

"If you're worried—"

"Kaylee and Nic live a few houses away." It's the reason I agreed to come all the way out here. If things go south, her house is only a short walk away. "I like this better than some fancy dinner in a restaurant."

"You do?"

"All those people gawking, trying to figure us

out?" I shake my head. "No thanks." More than one date in my past has gone south as people stared, no doubt trying to understand why a curvy woman like me was out with a guy way out of my league. Mitch is hot enough to turn *every* head. Add to that his family reputation...I didn't need the embarrassment.

"There's still a fancy dinner inside. But I'm making it myself."

"*You* cook?"

Mitch winks me at me, sending instant tingles straight to my core. "I'm more comfortable on the grill. C'mon. I won't bite." He pushes open the door "Unless you *want* me to."

A thrill races through me at his suggestive words Celia made sure that every article of clothing I wore tonight served one purpose; to help me get laid. I don't know why she's so focused on my sex life. She's the one binge-watching Netflix and nursing a hangover from too much wine last night.

"Your house is stunning," I say once inside unable to keep from scanning it all. The vaulted ceilings, the logs, the floor-to-ceiling windows. But it's a glimpse of his kitchen that captures my full attention.

"Go. Check it out."

Everything about that kitchen is heaven. The double ovens, the gas range, the granite countertops and so much prep space.

"Do you like it?" While I was busy gawking

Mitch managed to sneak up on me. He's standing so close that I feel the heat radiate from his body. I yearn to fall into his arms. To repeat those sultry kisses from the elevator.

"I love it." I'm unable to move from my spot, entranced by those dark eyes. His lips are so close. I've longed to feel them against my skin every waking minute. I've never felt such an intense attraction to a man before. Maybe Celia's right. I *should* have a little fun.

Mitch reaches out a hand to tuck my hair behind my ear. "If you keep looking at me like that, I'll never get the steaks on."

"I thought we might skip right to dessert."

Our lips crash together. Tongues tango. Hands greedily sweep our bodies.

I want this man more than I've ever wanted any other, and it's not just the dry spell. It's Mitch himself. I should run far, far away before he becomes any more irresistible. My resolve to keep my heart guarded is weakening. I want to give myself to him, and not just my body. My heart and soul, too.

I might be in trouble.

Mitch's hands slide up my arms and down onto my breasts. He squeezes them through the fabric, causing me to moan. It feels so damn good to be touched—desired. "Why don't we take this to the bedroom?" he growls against my ear.

"Okay." I hope he can't hear the shakiness in my

voice betraying just how nervous I am. I've had sex before. That's not the issue. I just don't remember enjoying it. I'm worried he'll be disappointed.

"Hey," Mitch says, tilting my chin up with his knuckle. "We don't have to do anything you don't want to. I promise my intention was to make you dinner and see where this night went from there. Skipping to dessert—"

"—Was my idea." I play with the hair at the back of his neck. Shyly, I admit, "It's been a while, Mitch."

"I'm going to take great care of you, Lainey." He kisses my cheek. In seconds our lips reconnect, hungrier than before. In a drunken tango, we end up down the hall and land on a plush bed. We tumble on top of the covers, losing clothes along the way.

My nervousness is subsiding to pure lustful desire.

I need Mitch to touch me. To feel him inside me.

"This is nice," he says, eyes fixed on my black lace bra. Seconds later, I feel the clasp give. "These are nicer." He gathers one breast in his hand, pushing my nipple toward his mouth. It feels likes heaven. I let my eyes fall closed as he suckles one, then the other.

We roll again, and Mitch's desire for me is no secret. I feel his length pressed against my belly. He's *huge*. I should be terrified that the man might split me in two, but instead I'm thrilled. "Mitch?"

"Yes, babe?"

"I want you inside me. Please."

"Since you asked so nicely." My panties are off in seconds. Mitch hovers over me, his hand priming my pussy. "Do you want me to use a condom?"

I bite my lip, debating. I know it's the responsible thing to do, but I also can't imagine having anything between us. I need to feel *all* of him. "I'm on the pill," I say, widening my legs in invitation. "I haven't been with anyone in years."

"I'm clean," he says, lowering his cock to my entrance. "I promise, I'll go slow." Mitch nudges his head into my channel. I gasp as he stretches me. "Look at me, Lainey. Keep your eyes on me. I promise I'll never do anything to hurt you. Okay?"

"Okay." I keep my eyes locked with his as he fills me inch by inch. My walls stretch, discomfort transforming to pleasure. His slow strokes pick up speed, the pace perfect. I can't believe sex feels *this* good. I let out a giddy, disbelieving laugh.

"What's so funny?"

"I didn't realize sex could feel so *good*."

"We've hardly gotten started." He kisses me hard on the mouth, increasing his pace to prove his point. My hips rock to meet his thrusts, amazing me more and more how good all this feels. I understand why my sisters are so smitten with their husbands now. Have I been missing out on this all along?

Mitch slips a hand between us, teasing my clit with his thumb. It's enough to escalate everything. I cry out his name. The same mounting wave of pleasure I felt build in the elevator is twice as powerfu now. This one is going to rock through my entire body. "I'm coming," I cry out.

Mitch pumps harder and faster until my body feels like it's exploding into millions of tiny pieces I've never experienced anything like it. "Wow. Tha was incredible."

"Good."

"Did you—"

"Not yet. I'm saving up for round two."

8

MITCH

Being with Lainey is everything I thought it would be and so much more. It was all I could do to keep from coming inside her, claiming her for good. Before I do, she needs to know what it'll mean.

Because once my seed is planted in her depths, there will never be another for me. I'll never give her up.

I'll love her until the end of time.

"How was your steak?" I ask, admiring how sexy Lainey looks wearing one of my t-shirts. And nothing else.

"Delicious."

"Good." My dick is still hard, begging for release. But both our rumbling stomachs overruled an immediate round two. Now that our plates are cleared, I'm ready for more. "Will you stay with me tonight?"

"I want to."

"Your friend?"

"Celia's only in town until tomorrow night." Lainey's eyes drop to my boxers. "I'm not going to leave you like that you know."

My dick will no doubt be in some state of semi hard from here on out where Lainey is concerned. I'm disappointed she can't stay tonight, but I understand. I'd never want to come between her and her friend. "Are you ready to go again?" I ask, clearing the plates.

"Yes." I watch her peel off my t-shirt, revealing all her curves. I love each and every one of them. "I thought we might have this dessert in the kitchen."

I flash her a smirk as I drop my boxers. "Come to me, Lainey. I want to bend you over and fuck you."

Her eyes darken as she approaches me, slipping between me and the sink. She arches her back and widens her legs, gripping the counter. "I'm ready Mitch. Take me. Come inside me."

I growl at her words. It takes every ounce of restraint to hold back long enough to lay it all on the line. "If I do Lainey, you're mine. I won't share you and I won't live without you. Is that what you want?"

"Yes."

Lining my dick up at her entrance, I push inside

in one swift motion. Reaching around her waist, I pleasure her clit as I pummel her over and over. Everything I've been feeling and everything I've been fighting is all coming to the surface now. I'm falling in love with Lainey Belmont. I'm falling hard. "Come with me, Lainey."

Our worlds explode together as I hold my cock inside her sweet channel. Filling her. Claiming her. Now and forever.

During dessert—strawberry cheesecake—I try to find the words to convince Lainey to stay the night. It doesn't feel right for her to leave after what just happened between us. But if I'm being honest, it doesn't feel right to sleep without her ever again. I want her in my bed, always.

"I wish you could stay," I finally say, knowing the words won't be enough. The fact that she's already redressed speaks to that.

"I need to check on Celia," she says, apology in her voice. "Mitch, it's not that I don't want to stay. I do." Still, I hear the hesitation in her voice. Something is holding her back. I remember her sister's words and wonder what I could do to change her mind. To make her believe she deserves a man who'll capture the moon for her. *I'm that man.*

"I meant what I said earlier," I say. "You're—"

"Hello?" Mother's voice echoes in my entryway, causing my blood to freeze. What the hell is she doing here? "James, are you home?"

Lainey's eyes widen, but before I can tell her this wasn't my doing or apologize for the interruption, Mother bursts into the kitchen.

"What's this?" Mother's eyes laser focus on Lainey.

"Mother, you interrupted a date. Is there an emergency?"

"Look here," she says to Lainey, ignoring me completely. "I know who you are. My son does not need some gold digger after his inheritance. If you think he's going to hand over a dime for your bakery, you're sorely mistaken."

"Mother!"

Lainey pushes up from her seat, grabbing her purse and dashing toward the front door. It all happens so fast I hardly have time to register it. I chase after Lainey, calling for her from the driveway. But she races toward Nic's house. I doubt Kaylee will be kind to me if I follow Lainey all the way there.

Instead, I turn back to deal with my mother.

"Sometimes you just have to call them like you see them," she says, helping herself to a piece of cheesecake.

"You need to leave."

"Excuse me?"

"You just chased off the woman I *love*."

Mother drops her fork and it clatters against the plate. "Love?"

"Yes, I love Lainey Belmont."

"You can't possibly—"

"I do." I'm trying like hell to calm my erratic, heavy breathing. "I get why you're being so pushy about me working in a garage, but you have no right to dictate my love life. Lainey doesn't care about my money. In fact, I almost lost her because of it."

"I had no idea you felt that way about her."

I finally take a seat and let out a heavy sigh. "I want to marry her. And if you ever want to see me take over Anderson Auto, you *will* fix this. If you don't, I'll resign right now."

"You wouldn't."

"I would."

It's not often Mother is shaken, but she definitely is now. After a few moments of strained silence, she finally says, "I'm sorry, Mitch. I had it all wrong." Mother has always been a force to be reckoned with, but she's always admitted when she's wrong. "I'll make this right on my end. I promise I will."

I just hope it's enough to win Lainey back.

9

LAINEY

"I can't keep up with all these orders!" Hannah emerges from the office holding a notepad. She's filled an entire page. "Biweekly cupcake delivery to the community center, monthly ice cream social at the elementary school, Friday donuts at Anderson Auto's corporate office *and* their garages in town."

The words *Anderson Auto* are the ones that resonate. "What?"

"You did say Anderson Auto, right?" Kaylee asks, hands on hips. She's been a godsend since Celia left town. She confessed that she was the one who gave Mitch my number, hoping he was different. She's been the shoulder I've cried on every night since.

The problem is that Mitch *is* different. But I'd

never risk Alice Anderson's wrath. What good is love if it costs my family the business we've built from the ground up?

"Yes, Alice herself is placing all these orders. They want to give back to the community through baked goods."

Kaylee stares at me until I meet her gaze. "Do you know anything about this?" she asks.

I shake my head. I've ignored calls from Mitch and fought the urge to listen to his voicemails. But I think it might be time to hear what he has to say. If Alice is placing all these orders with our bakery, it might be a peace offering. "I need to take a break."

All my sisters stare at me like I've grown three heads. "We didn't realize you knew what that word meant," Becca teases.

"Ha, ha." I snatch my phone and slip out the back door. I'm about to listen to the first message when I see him. "Lurking in a dark alley these days?" My words are wobbly and awkward. Not exactly the punchline I was going for.

"It's not dark yet," Mitch replies with a shrug. His smile is weak. The closer he gets, the more obvious it is to me that the man hasn't slept very well. *Is this my fault?* "I've been trying to call you."

I lift up my phone. "I was just about to listen to your messages."

"I can sum everything up for you right now." He takes the final step, leaving hardly a feather's width

between us. "I'm so sorry for what my mother di[d]
and what she said to you. She owes you an apolog[y]
and is ready and willing to give you one when you'r[e]
ready."

I feel a lump rise in my throat and try to clear i[t]
away. "Is that it?"

"No." Mitch tucks my hair behind my ear, th[e]
graze of his fingertips starting a replay reel in m[y]
mind. "I love you, Lainey. I meant everything I sai[d]
that night at my house. You're it for me. I've bee[n]
miserable without you."

"I'm sorry I ran off," I say, realizing I owe a[n]
apology too. "When your mother threatened th[e]
bakery, I couldn't stay. I had to protect my sisters."

"I understand." Mitch dips his head, our lips no[w]
a mere inch apart. "I promise Anderson Auto will b[e]
nothing but good for Sprinkles on Top. And [I]
promise to be nothing but good for you. You deserv[e]
the best of everything, Lainey. I'm prepared to lov[e]
you all the days of my life."

"What are you saying?"

"I'm saying I want you to marry me. Be my wife."

I wrap my hands around his neck and yank hi[s]
lips the rest of the way toward mine. Our kiss i[s]
hungry and filled with urgency, desperate to mak[e]
up for all the lost time. "Yes," I say between kisse[s]
my heart full. "Yes, I'll marry you."

EPILOGUE

FIVE YEARS LATER…

LAINEY

Today marks ten years since my sisters and I opened Sprinkles on Top. Business is booming better than ever.

"Is the cake ready?"

I shoot Kaylee a warning glare as I lean in, ready to apply the final touches. "Close."

"Can you believe we did it?" Kaylee rests a hip against the counter, admiring my cake. I'm too happy to scold her for interrupting and she knows it. I remember the first day we opened the doors, how excited and terrified we all were. Each of us gave our all, knowing our business might fail.

"Ten years," I say, still amazed time has flown so quickly.

"Look how much has changed for all of us," Kaylee says, sighing dreamily. "Five Belmont sisters, all happily married with new last names and a gaggle of kids."

I thought I was destined to be an aunt-only until I met Mitch. I rub my belly, thrilled at the thought of meeting our second daughter. There's always been one family with five daughters for as many generations back as we can find. My sisters think I'm the one destined to carry on our tradition.

Secretly, I hope they're right.

"Hey babe, how's that cake coming?" Mitch asks. "Huge crowd gathered on the street."

"And that's my cue to go." Kaylee heads for the doorway, saying over her shoulder, "I'll tell them the cake is coming."

Mitch kisses me on the back of the neck. Even after all this time together, my husband still makes me shiver with anticipation at the slightest touch. At this rate, we'll have five daughters in no time. "I've been dying to get you all to myself all day," he growls against my ear. I feel a breeze where Mitch gathers the fabric of my dress. "You've been working so hard on this celebration." His fingers tease my pussy through my panties. "Let me help you unwind."

"Mitch!" We might be interrupted at any moment. I could live with the embarrassment if one of my sisters caught us. But the idea that our daugher, or any of my nieces or nephews, might walk in us s too much to risk.

"Mother is taking Olivia for the night," he says, withdrawing his hand and fixing my dress. "When his celebration is over, you're all mine."

"I hope that's a promise."

"You bet it is."

"How about that cake?" Eliza calls from the doorway. "Is it ready *now*?"

Mitch and I exchange a heated look—a promise of what's to come tonight with a house all to ourselves.

"Lainey!" Eliza calls again.

I take one last assessing look at the masterpiece 've created. "It's ready."

STAY IN TOUCH!

Sign up for Kali Hart's newsletter to stay up to date on new releases, giveaways, and more!
http://eepurl.com/gHPmaf

Join Kali Hart's Reader Group on Facebook:
https://www.facebook.com/groups/1106383086217315/

Visit Kali Hart's Website:
https://www.authorkalihart.com

Follow Kali Hart on BookBub:
https://www.bookbub.com/profile/kali-hart

Follow Kali Hart on TikTok:
@kalihartauthor